Olivia picked her chair up and sat. Sipping her coffee, she watched him a few seconds. "Okay then. Talk," she finally said.

"I was military intelligence for a number of years, so if it's something where you need help in that direction, I'm your man. If you need someone with weapons skills, I'm your guy there, too."

"Why would you think I need that type of help?"

"Since you got so offended when I made the comment about your mother's illness, my training tells me there's something else going on here than a mere fear by a daughter of being held back by her mother's issues. Why don't you tell me what *is* going on and let me see if there's any way for me to assist you."

"Answer one question first."

"What's that?"

"Why? Why are you so gung-ho to help me? We've never really hit it off and, all of a sudden, you're being kind and want to act like the Boy Scout who helps the old lady across the street."

The phone started ringing again. They let it play out. Rocky picked up where they left off. "I want to help you because I'm a nice guy, no matter what you might think, and I see you need it. There's a mob outside your door who would eat you alive if given half a chance. You could call Sharon to assist you, but I'm quite sure my skill-set is a bit better at handling those people out there than hers."

"You're probably right, but can you blame me for doubting your motives?"

He shook his head. This was getting ridiculous. "You're right. I'm done. Have a nice life." Rocky rose from his seat, shoved the chair under the table, and turned toward the back door.

The moment his hand touched the knob, she said, "Okay. Okay. Sorry. I *do* need help. Please come and sit. I'll tell you everything."

New York heiress Olivia Jacobs flees from her stepfather who's trying to kill her in order to obtain her trust funds. Eventually landing in Texas where she buys a country bar she names *Ollie's*, Olivia believes herself safe. Then one night in the bar, some thugs decide to rob the place. Olivia pulls out her Stillson wrench and ends their plans. Unfortunately, the event goes viral on the internet, and the media surrounds her home the next day. Her cover is blown, and her face is all over the tabloids. Now she must run again. Rocky, a rancher living in the same town, offers to help her escape. Not quite trusting him, or the attraction she feels for him, she's reluctant—that is, until her stepfather's minions show up and she realizes she's out of options. Now both she and Rocky are on the run from one of the most powerful men in New York, and things are about to get ugly…

In *Cowboy Boots on the Ground* by Sherry Fowler Chancellor, Olivia Jacobs is on the run from her stepfather who is after her money. If she dies, her trust fund will pass to her mother who is in a coma and barely alive. At the moment, Olivia's hiding out in Texas where she bought a bar she calls Ollie's. When some thugs try to rob her bar, she defends herself, her customers, and her property with a wrench and ends up in a video on the internet. Now her stepfather knows where she is and will be sending men to dispose of her. So she has to run again. The only man she can trust is a former army intelligence soldier with whom she has a mostly hostile relationship. Will his skills be enough to save her, and why should he bother when he doesn't even like her? The story is suspenseful, intriguing, and the romance sweet. While classified as a romance, the story could also be classified as a thriller, since you'll be riveted from beginning to end. ~ *Taylor Jones, The Review Team of Taylor Jones & Regan Murphy*

Cowboy Boots on the Ground by Sherry Fowler Chancellor is the story of a New York socialite and heiress, Olivia Jacobs, who has been in hiding for years. It seems her stepfather has put her mother in a coma and is now trying to kill Olivia so that her trust fund will pass to her mother, whose death will then give the stepfather the whole pot. Olivia knows that once she dies, her mother won't live long either. She ends up in a small Texas town and buys a bar called Ollie's. She loves it there and hopes to be able to stay until she's thirty, at which time her trust fund will be transferred to her control and she can remove her mother as her beneficiary, hopefully saving both their lives. But when the bar is robbed one night, Olivia ends up on the internet and now everyone knows where she is. She has to run again before her stepfather and his men show up to dispose of her. Her only option is to accept the help of local rancher and former army intelligence officer Graham Rockford, an insufferable man who has been a thorn in her side the whole time she's been there. He could tell she's not what she pretends to be and has been suspicious all along. But without his help, she's doomed. Can she swallow her pride and accept his offer of help? And even if she does, how can one lone former soldier with demons of his own defeat the most powerful man in New York? *Cowboy Boots on the Ground* is both a sweet romance and a chilling thriller. Combining suspense, intrigue, and romance, the story will both warm your heart and keep you glued to your seat. Another jewel in the crown of this talented author. ~ *Regan Murphy, The Review Team of Taylor Jones & Regan Murphy*

Cowboy Boots on the Ground

Sherry Fowler Chancellor

A Black Opal Books Publication

DEDICATION

To my father, Donald Fowler, who doesn't like the phrase "boots on the ground" because the truth is, there are people out there in danger, not boots.

Chapter 1

A view of tumbleweeds and no trees, instead of shades of red and orange fall foliage out the window, depressed Olivia Jacobs more than anything else about this God-forsaken corner of western Texas. Well, maybe not more than anything, but it sure ran a close second to whatever else she could think of that she missed about early November in New York. Only a little over two years until she could go back. Surely those years would pass faster than the last five. They *had* to, right?

She stifled a snort. She must be the only woman in history to ever want her twenties to pass as fast as they could.

"What's with the sad face?" Sharon Brooks, her best friend, asked.

"Nothing." Olivia shook off the glums that had taken hold of her. "Just hoping that no one picks that song today."

"You crack me up about that song. I know you hate it for some reason."

"You have no idea." Olivia scrubbed the top of the old mahogany bar with a ratty old bar towel, making a mental note to purchase some new ones. This might be a hole in the wall place, but it didn't have to be grungy.

"Since this is your bar, I don't know why you don't take the stupid thing out of the jukebox."

"How quickly you forget. Remember the near-riot when I did?" Olivia gritted her teeth at the memory of the rowdy patrons of this honky-tonk bar she bought when she landed in town two years ago.

She'd immediately set about changing some things in the place and got a lot of flak for it, but that one song she despised got the biggest reaction when she took it out of play.

"I still can't figure out why you wanted to own a country bar when you hate the music. You have to admit, it's weird."

Olivia couldn't tell Sharon the truth. No one could know why she was here and why she chose such a place to hide. Maybe in two years when she turned thirty, she could tell the real story to all those people she'd been lying to about herself.

"It was available, and I needed a way to make a living. It's as simple as that."

Her friend placed an elbow on the bar and leaned close. "I don't believe you. You could've gotten a job anywhere with your brains. Owning this joint wasn't the only option. And I know Buzz didn't sell out cheap, so if you needed money, how'd you pay for this?" She sat up and opened her arms to indicate the bar as a whole.

"There's this thing called a mortgage. Perhaps you've heard the term?" Olivia winked to show she was kidding.

"I heard Buzz say you paid cash."

"Buzz is full of hot air." Olivia wanted to throw up. Why all these questions now? She'd been here a while and thought everything was going well. Yes, she did pay cash, but the previous owner wasn't supposed to tell. She hated small towns. Gossip, gossip, gossip. And she'd thought the grand dames of the Hamptons were bad. They had nothing on these people.

"You know I'm here for you if you need me, right?" Sharon leaned forward again, so intense, Olivia stepped back in fear.

"What do you mean, *need* you?"

"Oh, I don't know." Sharon shrugged. "In case there's a problem."

"I don't mean to sound cranky but what makes you say this now?" Had Sharon somehow heard something about her past? Terrified that she'd have to run again, Olivia tried to make her voice casual but was afraid she was failing in her effort.

Tex, a burly man known for drinking way too much, slammed his beer mug on the oak bar. "Hey, Ollie. I need a refill."

Olivia took the stein from his hand knowing it was his third but checking to be sure he did. "How many is this?"

"Three. Then I'm done. Mabel wants me home early for the grandkid's birthday."

"All right but someone's driving you, right?"

"Now, honey, you know this big old belly can handle more than three beers and still get behind the wheel."

"Nope. I'm not going to be sued when you take someone's life." Olivia clicked her fingers over her head and called out, "Hey, Sam, can you take Tex home when he finishes his beer?"

"Sure thing, Ollie. Add it to my tab."

She and Sam had a deal. He didn't drink much during the week and drove patrons home, and on Sunday afternoon, she paid him in whiskey—usually a bottle of Kentucky Bourbon—and he drank it at home. Keeping drunks off the road was something she decided she wanted to do as soon as she bought the bar. Sam lived within walking distance so she didn't worry when she gave him his pay that he'd be on the road.

"You're really something," Sharon said after Tex had his drink and wandered off. "I've never seen anyone care so much about the customers."

Olivia shrugged. "What can I say? I don't want any drunk driving fatalities or injuries on my conscience."

Two college students stood at the jukebox. Young women. Olivia knew instinctively they would play the song she hated. "Can you watch the bar for a minute while I run to the office for something?" she asked Sharon.

"Sure." Sharon moved to the gate in the bar that lifted to allow the workers to go behind. They brushed shoulders as Olivia practically ran to the back of the building to her office.

She almost made it before the song started. Unlocking the door with shaking fingers, Olivia lurched inside as soon as she could get it open. Too late. Some of the words trickled down the hallway.

Flopping onto the ratty sofa that had seen better days, Olivia burst into tears. The song didn't always affect her this way, but sometimes it hit harder than normal. It had to be the fact that it was November and the holidays were coming. And she was in Texas. Alone and with no hope to go home for at least two more years.

And then fresh tears. Home wasn't really home anymore, was it? With her mother in a coma and her father dead, what was there to go back to? Nothing. But at least she wouldn't have to hide anymore. Age thirty. That was the goal. To get to thirty.

After indulging in a few minutes of weeping, Olivia abandoned her pity party and stood. She went to her private bathroom and freshened her makeup. Making a face when she saw how red her eyes were, she reached for the Visine.

Sharon was already asking too many questions today. Olivia didn't need her prying for the reason she had bloodshot eyes all of a sudden.

She returned to the bar and took her place near the beer taps.

Sharon moved back to her stool. "Guess who came in while you were gone?"

"I don't know. Elvis?"

Sharon shook her head. "You always say Elvis when someone asks you that question."

Olivia shrugged. "It's as good a response as any since the answer could be anyone from Sam to Tex to the pope."

"I somehow doubt the pope will make his way to this backwater."

"You never know. He might like a Cerveza."

"Do you even care who came in while you were gone?"

Olivia wrung out the bar rag. "Only if he or she is buying a round."

"It's your favorite customer, and I'm sure he's not treating everyone to a round. At least not in *this* bar."

Great. Graham Rockford. The man who everyone seemed to love but her. He rubbed her the wrong way entirely—with his motorcycle named Prudence and his ponytail that hung past his shoulders.

"What does he want?" Olivia asked.

The man himself stepped up. "How about a PBR?"

Olivia quirked her eyebrows. "Really? You like PBR?"

"Sure. It's an honest man's beer. Cheap and filling."

"Hey, Rocky. What's the plan on that ride tomorrow?" Sam asked.

"It's a charity run for the children's hospitals. All you have to do is pay ten dollars and donate a stuffed animal. We'll ride forty miles from one to the other and donate half the money and toys at one end and the other at the end. It's a lot of fun to see the kids pick out a companion to help them along in their treatment."

"I'll be there." Sam tapped his fingers on the bar and address Olivia. "Want to ride along with me? There's room on my trike."

"I can't. Need to keep this place running."

"The man everyone called Rocky plunked his money onto the counter and grabbed the beer she'd placed in front of him. "As always, Ollie of Ollie's Bar doesn't want to support the community. I'm shocked you even asked her, Sam."

Knowing he was riling her up on purpose didn't make it sit any better with Olivia. She had always supported charities. Hell, she'd been on committees since she was in junior high school but she couldn't afford to become high profile yet. Not until that thirtieth birthday. "I'll have you know I support this community. I merely don't choose to do it publically and ostentatiously."

"So riding a motorcycle to a children's hospital is ostentatious now?" Rocky took a long swallow from the Pabst Blue Ribbon.

Olivia wiped the beer she'd spilled on the counter when she'd opened the pop-top on the PBR. "When you make a big production of it, it is. Being subtle isn't a crime, you know." "

"Never said it was, lady. You're too prickly for my taste." Rocky set his can down and tossed an arm over Sam's shoulder. "I hear you got a new bike. Let's go check it out."

"Yeah. It's a sweet ride. Come on over, and I'll show you." Sam turned back to Olivia. "If you change your mind, let me know. Be glad to have you come along."

"She won't change her mind. And besides, even if she did, she can't find a stuffed toy before tomorrow morning." Rocky walked away and out the door, followed by Sam.

As soon as they were gone, Sharon said, "I think he likes you."

"Who? Sam? No way. He's sweet on Russell."

"No. Not Sam. Rocky."

"Uh, no. Did you not hear how he talked to me? How he always talks to me?" Olivia could scarcely believe Sharon's words. Graham Rockford had no use for her. Sharon was delusional for thinking so.

And Olivia didn't care for him either. Sure, the man was handsome and rugged, even with the scar that slashed across his cheek. His scruffy beard was sexy, even though it had a gap where the scar flashed through, but he wasn't someone who she could find happiness with. Her life was only on hold for now. When she returned to New York, much would be expected of her, and she would have to choose someone of her own set.

The thought made her want to wail and gnash her teeth as the song she hated and the man who broke her heart flashed through her mind.

Yeah, he was of her set, but he'd ripped her heart out and left her with the memory of a stupid country song that should be banned from the world. Before it hurt someone else.

☙

As soon as Rocky got to the parking lot, he let out the breath he'd been holding since the moment Ollie spoke to him.

Why did he allow her to affect him so? She was the owner of a dive bar and should be beneath his notice, but there was some quality about her that he couldn't put his finger on. The lady wasn't who she appeared to be, and it bothered him.

His instincts, long honed in military intelligence, screamed at him that the woman was hiding something. He couldn't let it alone. The mystery of her nagged at him and begged to be solved.

For a long time after he mustered out, he couldn't focus. He didn't want to leave the service, but his injuries and his blown cover required him to do so. 'He'd fallen into a deep depression.

Once he got involved at the children's hospital, he'd started to pull out of his funk. And now there was this woman to figure out. Was she a criminal on the run?

Once in a while, when she spoke, she enunciated in a clipped tone. One he'd heard many times with wealthy people, and truth be known, some of his own family. He'd been told by Buzz that she paid cash for the bar, so she had money from somewhere, but, for all he knew, she could've robbed a bank or maybe seduced an elderly man and fleeced him.

She was pretty enough to do that. Blonde, leggy, and with green eyes that shot sparks when she was angry. Which she seemed to be every time he got near her.

Did she sense he was onto her not being who she

pretended to be? Was that why she kept him at a distance like she didn't do with anyone else?

Sam led him across the gravel parking lot to his house behind the bar. "What's on your mind? You've been really quiet since we left the bar."

"I was thinking about the logistics for tomorrow. Sorry."

Sam laughed. "No worries. It's not like I expected us to have an in-depth conversation in the parking lot."

"I don't think I've had what you might call an in-depth conversation in years." Rocky knew exactly when he'd had the last long conversation in his life. When he'd last shared a deep part of himself. But he didn't like to think about that time. With effort, he buried it in the recesses of his psyche.

"Isn't that usually the way with us guys?"

"I've heard that from many a man's wife." Rocky snickered. "The fairer sex seems to always want us to share our feelings, don't they?"

"You're right. Thank God I'm not planning on acquiring one of those."

"One of those?" Rocky grinned.

"Yeah. No wife for me."

"Me either, my friend. I'm too much of a mess to want to have one of those. God knows, she'd want to *fix* me, and I'm afraid I can't be repaired."

"Can I tell you how many women have tried to reform me? That think I'd like women if they could only get their hands on me?"

Rocky laughed. "I can only imagine."

Sam was what women would call good-looking and the fact that he worked out all the time didn't hurt either. Rocky had seen every new gal who came into the bar size his friend up as if checking to see where she would fit.

"Like what I have is a disease they can cure with a pair of boobs." Sam gestured as if he'd grown a pair on his chest. "But come on, enough with the problems of women who want us. Check out my new trike." He pulled up the door on his garage, and the two men entered the building.

Rocky stepped over to a 1966 GTO parked in the back. "What is that sweet ride there? Have you been holding out on me?"

"Oh, that's Ollie's. She's been tinkering with it for a while."

"Ollie? Her? She likes old cars?"

"Seems so." Sam shrugged. "She had that thing towed here about six months ago and has spent hours on it. Doesn't have a place to work on it at her house, so I let her keep it here."

"That lady is full of surprises, isn't she?"

"Have you never seen her Stillson wrench?"

"I've seen it." Rocky smiled. "She threatened to use it on me more than once."

"You're one of those kind, huh?"

"Yep. That's me. A trouble-maker." Rocky ran his hand along the side of the black GTO. "I'd like to take a spin in that."

"Fat chance. Especially now that I know she's reserved a side of the Stillson for you."

"I know. No chance at all." Rocky cast a longing glance at the car then turned to check out Sam's motorcycle. "But let's see your bike."

It was a great ride. Red and black and shiny with newness.

"That's a big hoss. Do you know how to handle something with that much power?"

"You want the truth?" Sam asked.

"Nothing less."

"I'm scared to death of this thing."

Rocky shook his head. This was one fine ride, and the man next to him didn't seem like a biker. It was a puzzle why he'd purchase that much power for his first cycle. "Then why buy it?"

"I wanted to be part of the group so I went to the dealer and they talked me into this."

"Have you ever even been on one?"

Sam smiled ruefully. "Sure. Of course. I had to take that class to get the license."

"Oh Lord, man. We've got to get you in some practice if you're coming on the ride tomorrow. Tell you what, let me lend you one of my smaller bikes until you get the hang of it. We sure don't want to be visiting you in the hospital. Can you come out to my ranch and let me set you up?"

"As soon as I drive Tex home. I promised Ollie I'd get him home safely and I probably better go see to that now."

"Sounds good. Once you drop him off, come on over. I'm heading that way."

They left the garage. As they walked toward the front of the bar, Rocky said, "Did you just decide you wanted to start riding or was there another reason you want to be part of the group?"

Sam ducked his head as if embarrassed. "Another reason."

"Want to talk about it?" Rocky thought he knew what the other man's motive was and didn't want to embarrass him but he was genuinely curious why Sam would buy such a noticeable bike. Most men did that to attract someone who might already ride. Tempt them, so to speak.

"Not really but I believe Russell is part of the group, right?"

"Ah, I thought it might be something like that," Rocky said.

"And you're not offended?"

"Of course not. To each his own, man, to each his own. I'm all about finding what you need where you need it."

"I'll see you at your place in a little while? I don't want to embarrass myself tomorrow."

"I'll be there. Come on when you're ready."

They arrived at the front of the bar, the gravel parking lot crunched under their feet. "Are you coming in?"

"Nope. I think the proprietor has seen me enough for today. I don't know why the lady doesn't seem to like me."

"It is odd now that you mention it." Sam turned to the door. "She's usually the first to welcome people, but you do seem to set her off."

"That's why it's best I go on home now." Rocky stepped over to his bike. "Prudence and I will see you later." He started the engine and roared off almost before Sam could get through the door.

As he rode on toward his ranch, their last words ran through Rocky's head. If others were noticing the way Ollie treated him, it wasn't something only in his mind, after all. She really was trying to keep him at a distance, and all that did was pique his curiosity even more.

What was the lady hiding? And what kind of name was Ollie for a woman anyway?

Chapter 2

The next day, almost as soon as she got up, Ollie started getting ready for the after-party she'd decided to throw for the motorcyclists. The jibe by Rocky about her not participating in the community hit home.

She wanted to keep a low profile, and she still would, but she could donate some drinks for a worthy cause. She'd stay inside the bar and have her extra bartender cover the outside part of the event. No publicity for her but a way to give back.

Based on past experience, she anticipated the crowd to show up around three in the afternoon. She'd asked Sam to put the word out and, even though she knew not all of the bikers would come, she knew there would be enough people to make it a good gathering.

She hung around the house in the morning, doing her week's worth of cleaning. One thing about having the small cabin here was it was easy to keep neat and tidy. Not like the place in the Hamptons that needed a staff just to keep it dusted. No clutter ever stayed around there for sure.

Still, with her hair up in the raggedy scarf she'd gotten it off her neck with and in a pair of dusty old cut-offs, she decided to go work a little on her GTO. It was a way to relax and bring back memories of her father. Of course, her mother, the Hamptons maven, hated the hobby her dad had loved. She thought it was a sign of being common to want to restore old cars. One should have those things done for them if they wanted a restored auto. One didn't get one's own hands dirty.

Never mind that her father was the one who came from wealth. Her mother, having grown up in genteel poverty, was much more rigid about rules.

Olivia sniffed back the tears that threatened to spill over. This was a way to honor her father. Forget the rest.

Shaking off the glums, she left and headed to Sam's garage.

Glancing at the bar as she drove past, she noted a couple of cars still in the parking lot. One of them was Tex's. His wife would bring him back for it later today. It made her happy that she had a process for no one to get arrested for driving drunk from her bar. She guessed it would make her lawyer happy, too.

She puttered around with the GTO for what seemed like minutes but had to be hours as Sam came in, poked her waist, and startled her. She conked her head on the open hood of the car.

"Ouch."

Olivia rubbed the knot, already forming where she

parted her hair, and looked at her watch. She'd worked way longer than she'd intended. She needed to go get a shower and check on the details of the party.

"Sorry, I was too excited. Didn't mean to scare you but wow. What a day. I wonder why I didn't get a bike before now."

"I wondered if you went on the ride since I see your motorcycle here." She wiped her hands on the greasy rag she'd set on the fender.

"Rocky loaned me one of his."

"Why? This new one is already not running?"

"No, no. As soon as he saw the monster I bought, he decided I needed to start with training wheels."

"Probably a good thing." She laughed. "I'd hate to see your brains on the highway."

"You and me both." Sam walked over and peered inside the hood of the GTO. "Making progress?"

"Sure. I should have it on the road soon."

"Can I have the first ride?"

"Absolutely." She wiped the sweat from her face with the rag. It was surprising still to her how warm it was in Texas in November. "I better get home to take a shower before the crowd gets here."

"You look gorgeous, but I'm sure you probably don't want to show off that new make-up job."

Confused, Olivia shook her head. "What new make-up?"

"The grease spots on your left cheek and forehead," Rocky said as he walked into the garage. "Although it could set a new trend among the ladies."

Great. Why did the man always seem to see her at her worst? Funny how it didn't bother her for Sam to see her in her rattiest clothes but for Rocky to do so annoyed her. Maybe it was because he had a way of making her think she wasn't good enough. Why that would be was also a mystery. Why would she care about that?

"I somehow don't think even the women in a dive bar like mine would choose to wear oil smudges for beauty."

"First, I think you sell yourself short on your bar. It's not really a dive, is it? And second, you also don't put much faith in the men who come around here. Don't you know grease monkeys like us find the sight and smell of oil on a woman sexy?"

"Right. Sell me another line, Mr. Rockford." Olivia smiled to take the sting out of her words, but she was absolutely sure the man did not find her sexy in the least. He was having a joke at her expense as he always seemed to do.

"I'm not kidding." Rocky nodded at her. "That do-rag on your head is the hottest thing I've seen all year."

The man had the nerve to wink. Olivia's hand went to her head as she tried to remember what she'd tied her hair back with. Oh yeah. The one with the skulls on it. The one she'd bought when she first arrived in Texas and was trying desperately to fit in. How naive she'd been in buying kitschy clothes that were more stereotype than reality. But there was no use in throwing away perfectly good scarves, was there? "You got an extra dose of the sarcasm gene at birth, didn't you?" she asked.

"You two are like snakes facing off trying to see who can strike the other one first," Sam said. "We live in a small town just counting the locals. Can't you try to get along? You're both my friends, and I hate to see you always at odds."

"I love that you're such a peacemaker, Sam, and I'll try to be better. I'm not sure Mr. Rockford can restrain himself from picking on me, but I'll sure try to stop doing the same to him."

Rocky laughed. "You can't even stop long enough to say you're going to stop."

That laugh got under her skin—the one he'd been using around her since the day they met. Why he didn't like or trust her, she didn't know. She'd heard he had been in military school when he was a kid, and maybe it was merely that he didn't like any woman who appeared to be strong and capable.

Wasn't that the way they ran those schools back when he would've been a student? Weren't they all male then? She didn't care. Whatever.

"I'm going. Will I see you later at the party?" Olivia directed her words to Sam. She didn't care one whit if the other man showed or not.

"I'll be there. Taxi service and all." Sam pulled her to him in a side hug. "I want to tell you all about the ride today. It was perfect."

"Any progress on your project?" She smiled as she asked. Sam really wanted to ask Russell on a date but was too shy to just come out with it. He'd wanted to get to know him better first. Rejection hurt too much to risk a casual date. Olivia could certainly relate to that.

"Some. Yes." Sam cast a pointed look at Rocky. "I'll fill you in later."

"All right. I'll be back later, ready to listen to all the scoop."

She left by the open door, leaving the two men to their conversation. She *did* wonder why Rocky had come back with Sam to the garage since his ranch was on the other side of the freeway. They'd both ridden up on bikes so it wasn't as if Rocky was in his truck coming to retrieve the loaner cycle he'd let Sam use. Weird.

It wasn't her business, though. She let it go. Whatever they were up to was none of her concern.

℘℘℘

As soon as Ollie was out of earshot, Rocky made a face at Sam. "I don't know why I let her get to me. You have a point. She and I need to try to get along, if not because it's the neighborly thing to do, at least for the good of the community at large. With her bar being a central place for people to hang out—my friends among them—I need to make more of an effort to fit in and not rile her. She *is* a bit like a snake. All puffed up and ready to strike every time I open my mouth."

"In all fairness, Rock, you tend to nettle her. I think it's to see what kind of reaction you'll get. It's like a game with you."

"You're right. I can't figure it out, but for some reason, I like to get under her skin. Maybe it's because she always seems unflappable. I've never known a woman quite like her. One minute, she's in the middle of the action in the bar with that crazy wrench she uses for protection, and the next moment, she's like some prima donna who expects adulation from the crowd. I sometimes wonder how well she could do the royal wave that I've seen Miss America contestants do."

"She *is* different. I'll give you that. Everyone else in Texas has a gun, but not her. She has that Stillson wrench. I wouldn't be surprised to see her get some guy's nuts in the clamp someday."

Rocky covered his crotch in mock-horror. "I hope it's not me when it happens."

"With the way you're going, it *will* be you. And then what will all the ladies do?"

"It's likely they wouldn't care. This old scarred up man doesn't entertain much anymore."

"Come on. Time to head to Ollie's and get yourself a drink. A toast to the success of the event today. I was shocked at how much fun I had hanging out with the kids at the hospital. I've never done anything like that before." Sam led the way out of the garage and pulled the door down.

As they strolled around to the front of the bar, Rocky said, "You were definitely a hit with the children. You should consider volunteering there with me."

Sam stopped in his tracks. "You volunteer at the hospital?"

"Absolutely."

Sam opened the door. "I'd have never imagined that."

The smell of beer greeted them, and the fading daylight was even more pronounced as they entered the cave-like atmosphere of the joint.

"Because I look so scary?" Rocky asked with more than a little anxiety. He'd hesitated when first asked by one of the nurses read to the kids when he'd come home from Iraq a broken man, but it turned out to be the thing to bring him back to life.

He still sometimes worried that he might scare a child, though, with the big scar on his face and his massive build. Some days he felt like Frankenstein's monster. All that was missing was the bolts on his neck. Although he *did* have one scar on the side where one particularly nasty guy had tried to cut his ear off.

"No. Not at all. I just didn't see you as a guy who loves kids." Sam held his hands up in surrender. "Before you get mad about that, think about it. You're not married and you never talk about children, so how was I to know?"

Rocky laughed. "Keep it quiet. I have a reputation to keep up."

They took seats in the corner booth and placed their order when the waitress came over.

Once she delivered Rocky's beer and Sam's glass of wine, Sam asked, "When did you start with the Pabst Blue Ribbon?"

"I know it's a cheaper drink, but I had an army buddy I met with a few weeks ago, and that's what he had at his barbeque. Surprised at how good it was, I decided to stop being such a beer snob."

Sam fiddled with the stem of his wine glass. "I'm not fond of beer at all. I don't like how it fills me up."

"You're right. That can be a problem." Rocky turned to look behind him as he heard several people greeting the owner as she came in. "Here's Ollie now. I guess the party can start."

"I was sure she said she was going to keep a low profile and let the party happen out in the side yard. I wonder if she changed her mind."

"What makes you think that?"

"She's got a small army coming in behind her. I see several of the people who were on the ride today. If the party was supposed to be out there, why are they all coming inside? There's really not enough room."

"Let's go find out." Rocky stood and moved toward the bar. In the moment he realized Sam wasn't behind him, he glanced over his shoulder. "Ahh." He let out a sigh. Several of Sam's pals had joined him at the table.

Sam grinned at Rocky and shrugged.

"Now what?" Rocky said under his breath. He hated that it now looked like he was on a mission to speak to Ollie. He'd intended to hang back while Sam talked to her about the party and now he was on his own.

When he arrived at the bar, he addressed Sharon rather than Ollie as each lady stood at opposite ends from each other. "I thought the party was outside."

"It is. Ollie needed some help getting a selection of drinks out there and asked some of the men hanging around to come take some coolers and cans to the yard."

"I'll be glad to lend a hand."

"Sure. That would be great." Sharon handed a few can across the bar to Rocky. "Take these out."

"Doesn't seem like enough. Who's in charge out there?"

"No one. Ollie was out there visiting when she got here, but she's back in now. Probably for the evening. I'll check on them soon."

"Seems odd since she's usually pretty anal about people drinking too much."

Sharon pulled a draft for someone who'd walked up. "She still is. Don't worry about that. But if you're that concerned, why don't you hang out there and bring us back a report periodically?"

"I think I will. Can't be any less friendly out there than it is in here." Rocky pivoted on his heel and walked outside.

He plastered on a smile as he did, in case anyone was watching. He didn't want anyone to suspect he was angry at the way the owner and her friend treated him. Discipline in the face of any conflict was ingrained in him. Just because he was no longer in the service didn't mean the lessons went away.

Soon enough, he was legitimately having a good time. His friends from the motorcycle run that morning were laughing, talking, and partying. How could he not join in?

Once in a while, he'd notice Ollie or Sharon out in the yard. Sharon more than Ollie. It struck him as odd.

Sam said Ollie wanted to keep a low profile for the party. Why? It was her bar and her idea to throw the bash. *Who does stuff like that?*

Rocky wandered around from one group to another. After an hour, he was ready to go home but noticed several young men loitering around the door to the bar.

They seemed to be up to something. He couldn't put his finger on it, but something made the hair on his arms stand up. What were they doing?

The roughest-looking of the group opened the door then glanced at his companions and nodded, as if signaling them.

Rocky tried to catch up as they entered the building. He pushed on the door, but it was shut solid. He pressed against it with his shoulder. It gave an inch or so, but there was some pushback. Hmm. Was someone holding it?

His right hand went to the gun he had tucked in the back waistband of his jeans. Surely these guys weren't stupid enough to rob the place. Didn't they know most of these people would be armed?

Giving one big heave on the door, Rocky almost fell face first when the thing opened suddenly.

He stumbled in and, to his utter shock, found Ollie standing over the young man who he'd pegged as the leader. She held that wrench she always threatened people with when they got too rowdy.

All the customers in the place, who weren't part of the gang, were lined up along the far wall, watching whatever had happened.

The three younger men stood gaping at their leader who was on the floor clutching his shoulder and wailing.

"Can one of you call nine-one-one? I know you all have phones, and we need to have some police come haul this trash away." Ollie swung the wrench in the direction of the still-standing gang members. "Anyone else want some of this?"

No one moved. Rocky took out his phone and made the call.

He hung up and stepped over to Ollie. "I guess it's a good thing no one pulled a weapon."

"I did," she said.

"You did what?"

"I pulled a weapon." She held the tool up. "This is a weapon."

"I meant firearm." He grabbed her wrist. "And don't fling that in my face."

"No one is flinging anything. Believe me, if I wanted to put it in your face, I would."

"Tell me something I don't know. But you *are* lucky no shots were fired."

"No one shoots in my bar, Texas or no Texas."

"Are you really that naïve?"

One of the young men lunged toward Ollie. She whirled around and whacked him on the shoulder as well. He screamed and fell to the floor next to his pal.

Sirens blared in the distance, coming closer by the second. Rocky pulled his gun and pointed it at the other gang members. "No one else move."

"Put that away. Now," Ollie practically screeched at him.

Puzzled at her reaction, he ignored her at first. She came to where he stood and kicked him in the shin. His bad leg. In intense pain, he glanced up at her face. Intending to blast her for her actions, he stopped short when he saw the genuine terror on her visage. Was she *afraid* of guns? Really? It seemed strange that the woman who would face down punks with only a wrench would be so rattled by a firearm.

Yes, there was more to this lady than met the eye. He was going to find out exactly who she was and what she was hiding.

Chapter 3

Olivia couldn't believe how the day had deteriorated. So much for throwing a party to thank people for working a great fundraiser. Why couldn't anything go well for her for once?

And Graham Rockford decides to be Mr. Big Hero and pulls a gun? One thing she could not abide was guns, and here she was in the middle of her bar with two wounded potential felons on the floor and a man who wanted to shoot them.

To say nothing of the terrified patrons on the sidelines.

Sirens heralded the arrival of the police and, thank God, Rockford put his gun back where it came from.

The two men on the floor continued their yelling and moaning.

She thought she heard one threaten to sue her for damages to his broken shoulder. That almost made her laugh, but amusement seemed a long way away at the moment.

"What happened here?" the first officer in the building asked.

Many voices answered him at one time.

"Everyone sit," he called out. "We'll need a statement from each of you before you go home."

Olivia stepped forward. "I'm the owner. The two men on the floor, as well as the three over by the bar, tried to rob me. They need to be taken out of here as they're interfering with my livelihood."

"Yes, ma'am. I'll have them removed from the premises and to a cruiser. Then we need to start with you on taking statements."

This was not going to be fun. She'd done her best to stay under the radar while here, and now she'd have to talk about things she didn't want to. There'd be no way to be evasive while being questioned by the police.

As the men were hauled away, over the cries of the first one she hit, she called out, "One round on the house while statements are being taken."

She hoped that would go a long way toward restoring customer relations.

It seemed to. The volume of conversation went up as the waitress and Sharon went about filling orders.

Leading the cop in charge to her office, over her shoulder, Olivia asked, "Would you like some coffee? I keep a fresh pot in my office."

"No, ma'am. No need for coffee."

The officer followed her into her sanctuary. After she removed the pile of paperwork she'd placed on the couch earlier, he adjusted his belt where his weapon and a Taser hung and sat. She always wondered how heavy those things were but knew it wasn't the time to ask.

This was the first time she'd ever actually injured someone and was nervous about talking to law enforcement about it. She trusted that she was in the right—after all, it was her bar they'd tried to rob—but she'd heard a lot of tales over the years about how one's words could be twisted to be used against them. The officer looked like a nice enough guy but should she talk to him without a lawyer?

In her former life, she had a lawyer on speed dial. Never for criminal work but consulting counsel before making a move was something ingrained in her, and this was tough. Torn about what to do, Olivia waited for the officer to speak.

"Want to tell me your side of it?" he finally asked, after staring at her for what seemed like an hour.

"My side of it?" Her voice came out as a squeak. Did he think she would lie about what happened?

"Little lady, in my experience in this world, there's three sides to every story. His side, her side, and somewhere in the middle lies the truth."

"That seems mighty cynical to me, sir. As if you go into every conversation believing the other person is a liar."

"Didn't mean it like that." He took off his hat that was really a cowboy hat in disguise and wiped his brow. "But most folks tend to shade the truth to make themselves appear better than they are. Or less guilty, depending on the stakes, if you know what I mean." He placed the hat in his lap and gave her an expectant look.

Not sure how to respond, Olivia was relieved when there was a knock at the door. "Come in," she called.

As the door opened, the officer said, "This needs to be a private conversation."

She shrugged. "Sorry. I thought it might be another deputy."

Rocky poked his head in. "Can we see you outside, Sheriff?"

"What is it, Rockford? You interfering again?"

"No, sir, just trying to help the local men in green and khaki."

Rocky flashed a grin that Olivia had seen before. It was the sarcastic smile. The one she was usually the victim of.

"Right. Like I believe that." The sheriff stood and put his hat back on. "I'll be right back, missy. Don't try to go nowhere and don't concoct some tale with this one." He poked his thumb in Rocky's direction.

Before she could react and deny she'd ever conspire with the man who was the bane of her existence, the sheriff was out the door talking to Rocky over his shoulder.

Rocky poked his head back inside. "Don't talk to him without a lawyer. I just overheard that one of those punks is related to a deputy. They will 'small town' you if you don't watch out."

"Mr. Rockford," the sheriff called down the hall, "you wanted me out here. Don't you think you should come with me?"

"Remember what I said." Rocky disappeared from view.

Having no idea who to call as she hadn't met any lawyers since moving there other than the one who did the closing on the bar purchase, Olivia sat in stunned silence for a moment. Were they really going to try to railroad her? She'd only been protecting her bar and her patrons. Was she going to face charges? Her gut churned.

Olivia picked up the receiver and dialed several numbers before setting it back down. She couldn't take the risk of calling her corporate lawyer. Not from here. She'd been too careful in her communications with him thus far and couldn't afford a mistake now. Not if she didn't want to have to move again before her thirtieth birthday.

At a loss what to do, she sat for a few moments then pulled out her cell phone. Googling the contact information of a criminal defense lawyer, she almost pushed the link to dial the number. Before she could, Sam came in. "Rocky said you need a lawyer. I've got one of my friends on the way. Hold tight, okay?"

"Thank God. I was in a panic. I didn't know you had a lawyer friend."

"I do. He's not a country music fan, so he never comes here."

Olivia could relate. She wasn't so much a fan herself, but she could suppress her taste in music in the interest of staying alive. After all, a little Miranda Lambert was better than a grave, right?

And, truth be told, some of those songs *had* rubbed off on her.

Sam put his index finger to his lip. "Shh, here they come."

When the sheriff returned, accompanied by a deputy, Olivia said, "I have a lawyer on the way."

"Are you refusing to talk now?" the sheriff asked. "I got two boys on the way to the hospital, and you're responsible. It's better for you to chat with me now. I can work you a deal."

"I'm afraid not. I didn't do anything wrong, and I won't be railroaded."

"You need to cooperate. Who knows when you might make an emergency call and no one be available to come," the deputy said.

"Wait. Was that a threat?" she asked.

"The only threats around here are going to come from me," a stranger dressed in a pair of khakis and a polo shirt said as he walked in.

"Oh, Lord, Sheriff, she's done gone and called the meanest snake in the grass at the courthouse," the deputy said.

The new arrival held his hand out to Olivia, "Snake in the grass at your service."

Olivia clutched on to his with both hands. This was the man who could rescue her from a fate she didn't deserve. She could feel it in her bones. Insolent and sarcastic, he was just what she needed. At least she hoped so.

❡❡❡

Worried that Sam had contacted Miguel Castro,

Rocky stood outside the door to Ollie's office. True, the lady needed a lawyer, but Rocky wasn't sure Castro was the right choice. He was known for being a hot dog and taking crazy risks that may or may not be in the best interest of his client. The man was a show-boater. Rocky wished Sam hadn't made that call.

There was nothing to do about it now. What was done was done. Rocky entered Ollie's office. Everyone turned to look in his direction.

Castro was the first to speak. "What can we do for you, Rockford?"

"I wanted to see what was going on. I saw those guys outside before they came in and thought maybe I could help with the investigation. Give my statement first."

The sheriff tugged on the waistband of his pants as if the weight of his gun-belt was pulling them down. "No need, son. You might think you know more than us yokels because of your background, but I'm completely capable of dealing with this scuffle between a bar owner and some of her customers."

Ollie stepped forward. "Wait one second, you're characterizing this completely wrong."

"Shh, don't say a word," Castro said. "Nothing to incriminate yourself."

"Oh, good grief. Everyone get out of my office. If you want to take a statement from me, I'm not talking until I know there will be no charges against me." Ollie turned to Castro. "Go earn your fee. Listen to the other people as they give statements, and then let me know the next step."

"It don't work like that, pretty lady," the sheriff said.

"Stop calling me anything besides my name. Just because you're law enforcement, you don't have the right to talk down to me."

The woman reminded Rocky of some kind of avenging angel. Those green eyes sparked and practically spit fire as she glared at the sheriff. If Rocky knew the cop—and he did—he knew the sheriff had spent the last fifteen minutes trying to intimidate Ollie.

Glad she was strong enough to stand up to the bullying sheriff—why he'd be surprised after she whacked two dudes with a wrench he didn't know—Rocky smiled at her, trying to send her mental kudos for being so brave.

She glanced over at Rocky. "What are you smirking about? Glad to see me in the hot seat?"

"I wasn't smirking. I was being encouraging. The only thing I'm glad about is seeing you standing up to this guy." He hiked his thumb in the direction of the cop.

Castro stepped between Rocky and Ollie. "Stop talking to my client. She might say something she shouldn't."

"I'm not about to do that. What I am going to do is close my door and have a cup of coffee to settle my nerves." She stared at the four men. "And I may even add some whiskey to that cup so please, all of you, go about your business."

"I'd like to stay for a moment, if you don't mind," Rocky said.

"I mind," Castro said.

"Your permission isn't required, man. Just the lady's." If he had to manhandle Castro to get him out of the room, Rocky would. He needed a moment to chat with Ollie. Not that he thought she'd listen to him, but he wanted to warn her.

"Fine. Suit yourself but talk fast. I'm suddenly exhausted." She moved to her desk and flopped into the chair behind it.

He studied her face. She *did* look done in.

"This isn't over, missy. You still need to give a statement," the sheriff said as he retreated from the room.

"My name's not missy," she called out.

Rocky almost laughed but held himself back. Somehow, he didn't think she would be appreciative of his amusement. He loved that she wasn't intimidated by the man. If someone had told him the day before that she was capable of talking back to the sheriff, he'd have never believed it.

She had always seemed too meek and mild for his taste. True, he'd heard stories about her pulling out the wrench when anyone got rowdy, but he'd never seen any sign that she was the least bit able to actually wield it as a weapon.

Too bad he didn't get to see her in action earlier. Always arriving late to the rodeo. That was his luck.

Once the room was empty, Rocky took the seat across from Ollie.

"What did you need?" she asked.

"I want to help you."

"Why? You've never made any kind of move to assist me before." She rested her arms on the table. "Why now?"

"You've gotten yourself into a big mess." He held his hands up at the expression on her face. "Hang on. Let me finish." She shrugged, and he went on. "I know. I know. You were only protecting your customers and the bar. I agree you didn't act wrongfully. The problem is, you've got these local knuckleheads who are going to be trying to find a way to hang it on you and let the nephew of the deputy off the hook."

"I don't see how that can happen." It was her turn to hold a hand up to stop him from talking. "Yes, I get it that this is a small town, and I'm the outsider, but I also know I'm in the right. How can they twist this to make me the culprit? And besides, I have a lawyer now, thanks to Sam."

"About him—"

"What? Are you going to tell me he's not admitted to the Texas bar?"

"No. Of course not."

"Then what? What is your issue with Miguel?"

"He doesn't always have his client's best interest at heart."

"What's that supposed to mean?" Ollie stood and stepped over to the coffee maker. She poured herself a cup and added a dram of whiskey. Turning to place the mug on her desk, she held up an empty cup and waggled it in his direction.

"Sure. And with whiskey."

Once she poured for him and retook her seat, she took a sip, let out a sigh. "Tell me about Miguel Castro."

"He's a guy who is all about the publicity. You'll

see. He will have you all over the papers and won't care if you look foolish. He only wants to make sure they spell his name right."

"You're kidding me, right?" She'd gone white. "The papers?"

Puzzled at her drastic reaction, Rocky realized he might be very close to figuring out exactly what it was about her that nagged at him. For her to be so concerned about publicity, maybe he was on the right track to be suspicious of her.

He thought about that for a split second then realized she needed a friend right now and not someone looking to dig up intelligence on her.

"No. I wish I was. He's a whore when it comes to the press."

"I can't have that." Her hands went to her cheeks which now were flushed a bright red.

He stood, sure she was about to either pass out or go into cardiac arrest. What the hell was she afraid of? This couldn't be good.

Coming around the side of the desk, he knelt beside her and took one of her hands from her face. It was ice cold. "What's wrong?"

She shook her head. Tears welled in her eyes.

"You can tell me."

"No. It's nothing illegal. I'm not on the lam from criminal charges or anything like that." She let out a laugh that was more like a shaky bark. "I bet you'd love it if I were."

"You must have a pretty low opinion of me. Last

time I looked, I wasn't all about wishing lovely ladies ill will or harm."

"I guess that's comforting." She bit her bottom lip. "You have to admit, we haven't been the keenest of friends, so can you blame me if I find it hard to trust you?"

"No, I understand that and don't blame you for doubting I want to help. I really do, but I get it that I'm not the first one you would call on."

"At least help me with this. How do I handle— kindly, mind you—firing the lawyer Sam sent? I somehow think he won't take it well."

"You're probably right. Let me think on that."

"Do you think the sheriff will be back to ask me more questions tonight? I don't think I can handle it."

"He has his hands full with all the witnesses out there. I'm going to go out and see what I can find out. Stay here. Drink your coffee." Rocky grabbed his cup, took a sip, and turned to leave the room.

As he reached for the doorknob, she said, "Thanks."

He looked back. "Anytime."

"Let's hope there's no other time." Her smile was wan.

Stepping out into the hall, Rocky walked toward the main area of the bar, his head in a whirl as he tried to put all the pieces together. Ollie of Ollie's bar was an enigma, and he was determined to figure out what was what and try to help her if he could.

Chapter 4

As soon as Rockford was out of the room, Olivia put her head down and let the tears flow. After ten minutes, she sat up and wiped her face. Enough of the pity party. Time to buck up, as her dad used to say, and make some hard decisions.

She didn't want to move again and hoped this incident would blow over. If she could just keep Castro quiet or if the damage was limited to the local newspaper, maybe things could settle down, and she could go on with her life here. A girl could hope, right?

Someone knocked on the door. Great. What now?

"Come in."

Sharon stepped inside. "Got some bad news."

Olivia braced herself for whatever was to come. "What else can go wrong tonight?"

Sharon passed a cell phone over. "Check this out."

Olivia glanced at the screen. A video of her using the wrench on the first suspect played. She glanced up at Sharon then back at the phone.

"That's not the only one." Sharon made a face. "There's a whole slew of them. And they're getting lots of hits. A woman whacking a young thug on the shoulder seems to be some kind of entertainment on the 'net."

"Great. That's just perfect." Ollie slapped the phone down on the blotter on her desk. Her friend had no idea why she didn't want publicity, but she was sure to know this wasn't good.

Sharon chuckled. "It'll blow over. Heck, this might even attract new business. You might think about framing that wrench and hanging it over the bar as a tourist attraction."

Olivia knew her pal was trying to cheer her up, but all Olivia wanted to do was throw up. This was not going to go well.

It was only a matter of time before someone from home saw one of the videos and identified her. She was going to have to pack and leave. Like tonight.

Just when she'd become comfortable and gotten the GTO almost ready to drive. She would hate to leave her new friends as well as the car.

She hadn't allowed herself to settle in to any other place she'd lived in the years since she left New York. Now that she had, it was imperative that she get away in a hurry. Through no fault of her own. Damn.

She needed to get Sharon back in the bar so she herself could sneak out and get what she needed to survive a few days on the road. Olivia also needed to arrange to get the paperwork out of her safe deposit box to turn the bar over to Sam and Sharon. Execute her exit plan. The one she'd hoped not to have to use. So much for that.

Truly, all Olivia wanted to do was cry but she didn't have that luxury. Nope. Not today. Save that for tomorrow in a lonely hotel room.

"You know what?" Olivia set the phone down and addressed Sharon. "I suddenly find all the adrenaline I generated earlier has caught up with me, and I'm so exhausted I can't keep my eyes open. Would you mind closing tonight while I sneak out the back door and go home to bed?"

"No. I don't mind at all but do you need me to drive you? I can cover for you once I drop you off."

"No. I got it. No worries. I can make it those few miles." Olivia stood. She twisted the bar key off her ring and passed it over. "Put this on your own keychain. I've got an extra one at home. It's silly for me to have the only one. Lord knows it's a good thing we've never had some kind of issue with that."

"Your bar, your keys, right?"

"It's time I let go a little bit, right?" Olivia's heart was breaking. This was goodbye, and she couldn't say it to her friend. Couldn't let her know how much she'd meant to her. How she was the first person Olivia allowed herself to trust during this life on the run.

"I like you just as you are. Even with all your quirks and need to be in control at all times." Sharon winked, but her words hit home. Olivia had always held herself in strict control. What choice did she have?

"I'm glad there's one person on the planet who accepts me, flaws and all."

"Don't forget Sam. He's the same. Loves you for you."

"You're right. The two of you are the best a girl could ask for. I'm lucky to have you both."

Sharon clapped her hands together. "Enough with the maudlin sentiments. It's almost like we're never going to see each other again. Like tomorrow will never come."

"Yeah, I know. Silly, right?" Olivia faced the door before Sharon could see the tears. "See you later." She walked out, turned left out of her office, away from the main bar and out the back exit.

Holding it together until she got to her car, Olivia allowed herself the luxury of a good cry all the way to her house.

As soon as she was through the door to the small cabin she'd been calling home, Olivia glanced around. It was cozy and sweet, but she hadn't really made her mark on it. A few throw pillows and coverlets were all that belonged to her, and they could easily be left behind. It was amazing how light she'd learned to travel.

In the bedroom, she took the large rolling suitcase from the top shelf of the closet and tossed it on the mattress. She unzipped it and, moving swiftly, grabbed clothes off the hangers and tossed them haphazardly into the case. She'd fold them in a few minutes. Right now, she needed to expend some of the nervous energy that threatened to consume her.

She had to spend the night here in town because the bank didn't open until nine but as soon as she could get into the safe deposit box, she was going to put the place behind her as if she robbed the 7/11. Thinking about robbery reminded her. She hustled over to the closet again and crouched down. Lifting the corner of the old boot box stashed there, she pulled out a fireproof metal safe.

Returning to the kitchen with the box in her hand, she plundered in the back of the cabinet until she located a ratty old Tupperware container with an orange lid. Opening it, she rooted around in the elbow macaroni until her hand touched the key.

Inside the box was a wad of cash, some bearer bonds, and a fake passport she'd paid a lot of money to acquire, hoping at the time she'd never have to use it. So much for that. The day of reckoning was here.

She'd have to make a break for it.

A pain pierced her chest. She had to grab hold of the countertop to stay on her feet. God, she didn't want to go. Shocked at how this town and its people had invaded her heart, Olivia let out a moan of distress.

Getting a grip, she finally shook off her melancholy. After all, she could always come back if she made it to her thirtieth birthday. But would they forgive her for running off like a thief?

Deciding she could meet that hurdle when it arrived, Olivia carried the metal box to the bedroom, placed the bonds in the zipper compartment on the inside top of her suitcase, and started the process of folding her clothes. Periodically, a tear fell on a shirt or a pair of jeans, but she kept working. There was no choice.

∽◈∾

As soon as he got up the next morning, Rocky tugged on his jeans and the special order cowboy boots he wore now that one leg was a bit shorter than the other.

Once he was dressed, he drove his old Chevy to the bakery on Main Street. The place was abuzz as he entered.

"What's going on?" he asked the man at the first table. The line was long, and he'd have to wait a bit for his coffee and bagel.

"Check it out. It's about Ollie. Or should I say Olivia?"

Confused, even though he'd long suspected Ollie was short for some other name, Rocky took the proffered newspaper from the man whose name escaped him for the moment.

The headline read: *Poor Little Rich Girl Found in West Texas.* The sub-headline went on to say *Olivia Jacobs, Daughter of Amos Jacobs, Missing Since her Father's Death and Mother's Illness, Surfaces At Long Last. In a Dive Bar, of All Things.*

Shocked, Rocky scanned the article.

It wasn't what he'd thought about her, but it made a kind of sense now that he was reading what her life had been like.

Of course, nothing explained why she disappeared from her hometown, but at least she probably wasn't a criminal.

The article speculated Olivia—that name sure fit her better than Ollie ever had—had left because she was somehow responsible for her mother being in a coma.

Rocky in no way believed that. Sure, the lady could whack a pretty mean wrench, but she wasn't normally a vicious kind of person. He knew violent people and, if she had such propensities, he'd have seen it.

Determined to find out the whole story from the person who lived it, Rocky handed the paper back to the man and left the bakery without his breakfast. He could always eat later. Somehow, he thought she might be in need of a friend right at this moment.

When he arrived at her house, he was positive she needed someone to be at her side. There were a number of news vans out in the street. Reporters and cameramen milled around on the lawn, destroying what grass remained at this time of year.

Rocky was sure she was inside, probably in a panic if the way she was acting the night before was any indication.

Parking his truck in the driveway that was miraculously empty, he got out and made his way to the front door.

He was impeded every step of the way with reporters shoving microphones in his face. They shouted so many questions, in so many accents and tones of voice that it sounded like the cacophony of sound that usually rang out in school cafeterias.

At the door, he knocked and called out, "Ollie, it's Rocky. Let me in. I can help you."

The curtain at the side of the front window twitched so he knew she was in there. He presumed her car was in the garage since he didn't see it.

He pressed his lips to the crack in the door. "Open up. Quickly. I'll edge in."

In a few moments, the curtain moved again. He leaned against the door, ready to slide inside as soon as it opened.

Hopeful Ollie would trust him, he braced himself to act.

The door cracked. Rocky darted in and turned to look at her.

She was pale and looked as if she'd spent a sleepless night. He'd never seen her like this. True, she was normally a low-maintenance, jeans-and-T-shirt-wearing kind of girl—well, he'd *thought* she was—but she was always neatly turned out. She didn't have the expensive manicures of some of the ladies he'd dated but her hair was always combed and her clothes clean.

At this moment, the lady appeared to have spent the last week in the same clothing and her hair was a snarled mess.

"What are they all doing here? Is it the videos people took and put online last night?"

"You have no idea what's happened?"

"No." Ollie shook her head. "I don't have a computer, and I never got a television when I moved here since I'm usually at the bar."

"You don't have a computer?" This news stunned Rocky. Who of their generation didn't have all the electronic paraphernalia available out there?

"No. When you're trying to keep a low profile, computers can give you away." She sighed. "But come on.

Let's sit in the kitchen where I don't have to see those people out there. You can tell me what's going on and what I missed."

He followed her to the eat-in kitchen and sat at the table. She poured them each a cup of coffee. "Black, right?"

"Yes. Thanks for remembering." He smiled and, once she sat, he reached out and took hold of the hand she placed on the tabletop.

"I haven't seen a television today, but I saw a newspaper article."

If it were possible, Ollie turned even whiter. "What did it say?"

"That your name is Olivia Jacobs, and that you disappeared a number of years ago."

"And, let me guess, they accuse me of doing harm to my mother?"

"It's alluded to, yes." He let go of her hand and took a sip of his coffee. Watching her over the rim, he waited silently for her to process what he'd said. In his days as an interrogator, he knew it was better to let things come out slowly and naturally.

"I didn't." Tears welled in her eyes. "I'd never do anything to her."

"The article said your parents were divorced and you lived with your father."

"I did, but that doesn't mean I didn't love my mother." Olivia sat back in her chair and crossed her arms over her chest.

"You don't need to be defensive with me. I believe you."

"Wait. Haven't I always been defensive with you?" Her eyes narrowed. "Exactly *why* are you here?"

"I thought you could use a friend."

Before she could respond to his statement, the phone rang. Olivia stared at it.

"I'm not sure you should answer. It's probably a reporter."

"I know. It's been ringing all morning. I answered it once and thought it was a sales call when they said they were from the *New York Times*. When I said I wasn't interested in a subscription, the person said she was a reporter and wanted to talk about the incident in the bar." She shook her head. "Why it didn't dawn on me then that it was much more than a local story about the attempted robbery? It was like my mind wasn't processing what she said."

"You *do* look like you've been up all night. Maybe it's the sleep deprivation."

"What a nice way to put it. That I look like crap, I mean."

"That's not what I meant." Rocky leaned forward, arms outstretched, "I want to help you if I can. Tell me what I can do."

"I don't think there's anything you *can* do. I was leaving town as soon as I could get to the bank this morning but now that the whole world knows where I am, I don't know where to go."

"Why go anywhere? Why not stay? Keep running your bar?"

"It's not that easy."

"Why? What's complicated about it? So what if you decided to bail on your mom when she got sick? Some people can't handle that kind of thing. There's no shame in that."

She leapt up from her chair so fast, it hit the floor. "Is that what you think? That I *bailed*—as you put it—on my mother because the rich, spoiled girl couldn't handle a little too much reality? That her mother in diapers in a bed, being turned by nursing staff three times a day, was just too much for her that she *ran*? Is that really what you think?"

"I don't have any opinion at all. Why don't you tell me what the truth is?"

"I don't owe you an explanation." She stood at the table. Rocky didn't know if she wanted to smack him or throw him out. Or both.

He stayed in his seat. Maybe with her standing above him, she would feel in the more powerful position and trust him with what was going on. "No, you don't, but from where I am—on the outside looking in—you need a friend. To trust someone." He held his hand up. "I know. You have Sharon, and you have Sam. But let me tell you a little bit about my credentials. Even though you don't like me much, I think I'm in a position to help you move past whatever has gone on in your life to bring you to this place."

Olivia picked her chair up and sat. Sipping her coffee, she watched him a few seconds. "Okay then. Talk," she finally said.

"I was military intelligence for a number of years, so if it's something where you need help in that direction, I'm your man. If you need someone with weapons skills, I'm your guy there, too."

"Why would you think I need that type of help?"

"Since you got so offended when I made the comment about your mother's illness, my training tells me there's something else going on here than a mere fear by a daughter of being held back by her mother's issues. Why don't you tell me what *is* going on and let me see if there's any way for me to assist you."

"Answer one question first."

"What's that?"

"Why? Why are you so gung-ho to help me? We've never really hit it off and all of a sudden, you're being kind and want to act like the Boy Scout who helps the old lady across the street."

The phone started ringing again. They let it play out. Rocky picked up where they left off. "I want to help you because I'm a nice guy, no matter what you might think, and I see you need it. There's a mob outside your door who would eat you alive if given half a chance. You could call Sharon to assist you, but I'm quite sure my skill-set is a bit better at handling those people out there than hers."

"You're probably right, but can you blame me for doubting your motives?"

He shook his head. This was getting ridiculous.

"You're right. I'm done. Have a nice life." Rocky rose from his seat, shoved the chair under the table, and turned toward the back door.

The moment his hand touched the knob, she said, "Okay. Okay. Sorry. I *do* need help. Please come and sit. I'll tell you everything."

Chapter 5

When Graham Rockford—she'd always thought the Rocky nickname wasn't as nice as his real name—returned to his chair, Olivia refreshed their coffee and took a deep breath. Doing something she never dreamed she would do until she was safe, she opened her mouth to tell the story of how she'd gotten where she was. "When I was fifteen, my parents got a divorce. I adored them both. As an only child, I'd been close to each in a different way."

"I can understand that."

"I went to live with my dad. Well, actually, we stayed at our penthouse apartment on the Upper East Side and Dad also got the house in the Hamptons. He bought Mom an apartment in another building close enough to the one he and I were in so I could see each of them as often as I wanted."

"That was good. If people can't be together in a marriage, I think it's great if they can put their child's needs ahead of their own."

"Exactly." She nodded. "And it *was* good for a while. Until Mom met her new husband."

"Uh-oh. I've seen that mess up a good thing way too often."

Olivia took a sip of her coffee. "And that's what happened here."

"Things got bad then?"

"Yeah, you could say that. Mom's husband isolated her as much as he could from her friends and even me. Whenever I came over, he made excuses why she couldn't see me." She wiped a hand over her eyes. This was harder than she thought it would be to talk about. It was all flooding back. How her mother deteriorated almost before her eyes.

A touch on her hand brought her back to herself. "Sorry. I can see this is difficult for you," Graham said.

She couldn't help but think of him by the kinder, gentler name since he was being so nice. "It's all right. Let me just cut to the basics. Maybe that will be easier."

The phone rang again. She glanced up at it on the wall. "I may have to jerk that thing loose."

"Let it go."

When it stopped, she continued, "Dad died. Heart attack while I was in college—even though he'd had open-heart surgery earlier. When he was gone, I came into my trust fund. Well, partially. Before he died, he gave me an allowance. After, I got draws from my trustee."

"So far, I don't see anything that would make you run unless your mother was asking you for money."

"Oh, no. She never did. She had a fund as well that Dad settled on her."

"Then what happened?"

"Mom was still the beneficiary of my trust."

"So, she would get your money if something happened to you?"

"Exactly. *Now* are you getting the idea?"

"I think so, but draw it out for me."

"Mom's health started deteriorating almost as soon as Dad died. She got worse and worse, and then accidents began to happen to me."

"Like what kind?" He took a sip of his coffee and made a face. "Ugh. Cold."

"Want me to brew some more?"

"No thanks. Just tell me the rest of the story. What kinds of accidents?"

"Standard stuff. Brake failure, a gas leak, a hit and run rear-ender wreck and one near miss on a sidewalk where a car almost ran me down."

"And you think they weren't accidents, I presume?"

"I know they weren't just like I'm sure my mother's coma was induced by something injected by that man she married."

"Did you go to the police?"

"I tried." She nodded. "They didn't do anything because her husband said I was on a vendetta against him. There was no real investigation at all."

"So why did you disappear?"

"Things escalated for me when Mom went into the coma. More accidents happened, and I knew it was only a matter of time before I either died or was in a vegetative state as well. With Mom out of it, her husband was the one to administer her trust fund and if I were incapacitated or died before I turned thirty, she, as my successor would be entitled to my funds. He would have unfettered access to all the money."

"What's the magic about being thirty?"

"The way Dad set the trust up is that Mom would be my beneficiary until I reach that age. Once I turn thirty, I can name my own. He did that so I wouldn't fall prey to some gold-digger in my twenties. Mom had always said if I had children before thirty that she would change it from her name to my kids' names. She had no interest in taking my funds."

"She sounds like an amazing lady."

"She was. Is." Olivia's eyes filled with tears again as she realized she'd started thinking of her mother in the past tense. True, the lady had been a strict taskmaster and very particular about manners, but she *was* her mother, after all.

"So you wanted to stay on the down low until that monumental birthday, huh?" Graham asked.

"Yes. It was vital. And now this happened." She ran her hand over her cheek. "I feel doomed."

"Hopefully not. We can handle this."

"*We?*"

He nodded. "Yes, we."

She allowed herself to let a small amount of hope into her heart. After all, he had to know his way around a knife or two to end up with those scars. Well, she presumed so, anyway, and prayed the other guy had gotten the worst end of whatever that fight had been about.

"So, when is the big day?" He grinned. "Not that I'm all about asking women their age."

"In a little less than two years. I turned twenty-eight in August."

"I kind of remember that. That you had a birthday, I mean, not your age. Didn't Sam hang some streamers over the bar?"

"I think what you're remembering was the near riot from some regular customers when he blocked the television when they were watching some baseball game."

"*Some* game? Ha. That was the championship."

"Sorry. I'm not a fan." She shrugged. How they got off on this tangent, she had no idea.

"What was your plan if your stepfather ever showed up?"

"He's not my stepfather. He's the man who married my mother." She let out a sob. "And probably, ultimately, her murderer."

"All right. I won't refer to him as that then. What did you expect to do to protect yourself if he found you?"

"I was hoping by keeping off the internet and using a fake name that he wouldn't but in case he did, I have a fake passport and some money squirreled away."

"What about the bar? Were you going to abandon it until you could come back?"

"No, In fact, I was going to hand it over to Sam and Sharon to run. I planned to drive to the bank this morning and get the deed I've already signed to them out of my safe deposit box." Olivia glanced in the direction of the living room and front door. "With that pack of baying wolves out there, that's impossible now."

"Want me to go instead?"

"Can't be done. You'd never pass for me. Too tall, you know." She gave him a bitter smile. Would that he could go take care of that bit of business for her. She could then make her run for the border with a clear conscience.

"At least you're still needling me. All isn't lost yet."

She tried not to let despair rush over her. "It's pretty close."

A banging at the kitchen door startled her so much, she jumped a few inches in her chair. "Oh, God, they're coming in the back now."

"Ollie, Ollie, it's Sharon. Are you in there? Open the door."

Graham stood and walked to the door. He pulled back on the dimity café curtain and peered out. "It's her. Want me to open up?"

"Yeah. Let her in."

Sharon breezed in, out of breath. She darted to where Olivia sat and hugged her in the chair. "I've been frantic. Why didn't you answer the phone? I called and called."

"I was afraid it was another reporter."

"I've told you a million times to get a cell phone where you could have caller ID. If you had that, you'd have seen it was me." Sharon stood and leaned her hip on the countertop. "I finally had to get in my car and come over. It's crazy out there."

Olivia let out a bark of a laugh. "Tell me something I don't know."

"Oh, I will, I think." Sharon pulled out her phone. "Take a look at this."

She held out her phone.

Olivia and Graham angled toward the screen. Sharon pushed the play button,

A private jet landed at the airstrip. Olivia's ears suddenly seemed as if they were full of cotton. She could barely register what the news anchor was saying as the plane landed and the door opened.

As soon as she saw the young man who stepped onto the portable staircase from the door, Olivia let out a moan, and the last thing she remembered was the darkness descending.

☙❧

As soon as he saw Olivia going down, Rocky leaped from his chair. He caught her right before she hit the floor.

Scooping her into his arms, he carried her to the couch in the other room, trailed by Sharon. By the time he placed Olivia on the cushions, she was stirring.

Amazed at how quickly she'd gone from Ollie to Olivia in his mind, he knelt beside her and squeezed her hands. "Are you all right? What happened?"

"I'm sorry, I didn't mean to upset you. Who *was* that guy?" Sharon asked. "And what did he do to make you fall out like that when you saw him?"

"Let her catch her breath before you interrogate her," Rocky said.

"Don't tell me what to say to my friend. We were best friends before you ever met her. Who do you think you are to talk to me like that?"

He stood and moved away from the couch. "Wait one second. No one was trying to say you're not her friend. But now that you mention it, what kind of pal comes in and acts like she has a fun surprise and it's really a mean-spirited act of aggression?"

Sharon crossed her arms and stuck out her bottom lip. "Mean-spirited? What's that supposed to mean?"

"Stop. Both of you." Olivia sat up. She ran her hands through her hair, making it stand up even more than it had been when he came into the house.

"Sorry, but she waltzed in here and upset you more than you already were. I shouldn't have turned on her, but I'm worried about you. Have you fainted before?" Rocky asked.

"No, I can't recall a time I've ever fainted." Touching her brow, she added, "Was that what that was? Things went dark around the edges, and then I don't know what happened."

"You almost fell out of the chair. Rocky grabbed you before you hit the floor, thank goodness." Sharon tossed a small smile in his direction. He chose to take it as a kind of apology.

Olivia held her hand out. "Give me that again. I need to watch and try to hear what the announcer said. She sounded very far away when I saw the plane."

"You mean you recognized the plane? How can you do that? It's just a small plane. What do you know about those?" Sharon asked.

It was all Rocky could do not to say something again to the woman. How had he never noticed the way she went on without letting anyone answer her string of questions?"

"Come sit beside me a second." Olivia adjusted herself on the couch to make room for Sharon. She patted the cushion beside her. "I need to tell you something."

"What? You're scaring me."

"Don't be scared. I just want to let you know who I really am."

Rocky stepped over to look out the front window. He adjusted the curtain, but before he could peer around it, Olivia called out, "You, too, Graham. Come listen."

Sharon tilted her head as if confused. "Graham? Why are you calling him that? No one calls him that."

He stepped over to the sofa and sat on the rolled arm next to the end where Olivia was. "My mother does."

"Your mother does what?" Sharon asked.

"Calls me Graham." He smiled. "It *is* my name, you know."

"Then why do you always say you're Rocky?" Sharon asked.

"It kind of stuck when I was in college and then the military."

"You went to college?"

"I don't want to be rude, Sharon, but you can ask me anything you want about my history once we get Olivia's life back on track. Let's focus on her for now."

Sharon's head turned so fast in Olivia's direction, Rocky was afraid she'd get whiplash. "And so now you're going by another name as well?"

"Olivia is my real name. I'm sure if you've been watching the news all day like you said you were that you knew that," Olivia said.

"Yes, I heard that but why? And who was that man on the plane?"

"I'm trying to tell you." Olivia didn't seem to be losing her temper, but she was holding Sharon to a standard that Rocky couldn't seem to. Olivia knew how to handle her friend, for sure.

Sharon patted Olivia's thigh. "Then do it."

"The man who got off his plane—that I recognized by its tail number—used to be my fiancé. His name is Bradford Roché."

"Oh, God, you were engaged? What happened?"

"He broke it off." Olivia pushed her hair behind her ears. "You know that song I don't like to have played at the bar?"

"Yes?" Sharon asked.

"That was our song. Well, not really but it was the one he always said was ours."

"Why did you break up?" Rocky was glad Sharon asked the question. He was curious but didn't want to seem nosy.

"I don't really know. I got up one day, and there was a note on the dresser. When I opened it, it just said he couldn't do it anymore and was gone. In a panic, I looked in the closets, and he'd taken all his things and left."

"Man, that was rotten. I wonder why he's here now," Rocky said.

"No idea and I don't care. I never want to speak to him again." Olivia sighed. "He's not usually an attention hound so I can't imagine what he'd be doing here. It's odd that he *did* decide to come."

"Before Sharon got here, we were talking about what you wanted to do about your situation. I know you haven't had time to think about it, but we need to make some kind of decision." Rocky shifted off the arm of the sofa and moved back to the window. "I have a feeling we aren't going to be left in peace much longer. If not the sheriff, this Roché guy may show up."

"What are you two talking about?" Sharon asked.

"I've been in hiding for a number of years because my mother's husband is trying to harm me to get his hands on my trust fund."

"Whoa. You've been keeping that a secret?" Sharon asked.

"Yes, of course, I didn't want anyone to find me, so I never discussed it or my past in any way. This is why I don't have Internet access here. Not wanting to be found is a tough way to live, let me tell you."

"Now that you *have* been, though, are you going to try to hide again?" Sharon asked.

"I was going to, but I'm not sure how I can since I can't even leave my house."

"Here's an idea," Rocky said, secretly pleased she was calling him by his given name. It seemed to flow off her tongue nicely, warming his heart. "Let's have you switch clothes with Sharon. Since she has on that ball cap, if we went in her car, they'd think she was leaving, and you'd still be here. I'll take you to my ranch. She can come later and bring your car and suitcase. You can stay with me until this blows over."

"Good plan, except for two things," Olivia said.

"What's that?" he asked.

"First, it would be awkward to stay at your place." She held her hand up. "Don't get offended. You know we're both on new ground here. We've not exactly been friends, and now you're opening your house to me. It's appreciated, but it would be weird."

"And the second downside?" Rocky made himself not react. It was hard. After all, he'd gone to some trouble to come here to try to help her, and she was practically tossing it back in his face.

"It's not going to blow over."

"So, you're afraid you'd have to live with me forever?"

Sharon burst out laughing. "That's funny, Ollie. You know, this time yesterday, you'd have never been anywhere near considering such a thing."

"And you're all right with me dressing in your clothes and running off in your car?" Olivia asked Sharon.

"Sure. I know where to find you, and I seriously doubt you'd want to steal my car anyway. It's an old clunker Honda Accord with more rust than paint. Who steals those?"

Rocky squeezed her hand. "If you're afraid I'll put the moves on you, you needn't be. The place is vast, and I have a guest cottage as well as a full apartment in the basement. It even has a lock on the door."

He hoped he didn't sound offended, but he kind of was. All he wanted to do was help her, and he was being made to feel like he was some kind of pervert wanting to get her to his house and into his clutches—

He stopped himself. She'd never said anything like that. Letting an old battle from the past seep into the present wasn't kosher, and he needed to stop. It wasn't like he could force her to let him assist.

Deciding to back off entirely, he walked from the front window toward the kitchen.

When he reached the arced area leading to the other room, he turned to look at the two ladies. "I'm going home. It's been a long day already, and I have some livestock to tend to."

"So you're just going to leave?" Sharon asked.

"Yeah, I think so. I can't force Olivia to take my assistance. I'm not some kind of Cro-Magnon man, ready to throw her over my shoulder." He gave a tight smile. "The way I see it, Olivia has made it this far on her own and has trust issues, obviously. So, I'm stepping out. It's better in the long run anyway."

"What's that supposed to mean?" Olivia asked.

"I've been told on a number of occasions that I have a hero complex, and it's clear you have a victim complex. Clearly, this is *not* a good combination." He turned and walked out.

Chapter 6

That was more in keeping with the Rocky we all know, wasn't it? The getting testy about something you said or did and either lashing out or leaving, right?" Sharon asked.

"Yeah, but he's right. I wasn't being fair to him, was I?"

Almost as soon as the words were out of her mouth, there was a knock on the front door. Immediately regretting letting Rocky leave as she sure could use a big man around to chase off the rabble presumably now on her porch, Olivia darted a glance at Sharon. "It *has* to be a reporter, right?"

"Do they usually knock? I thought they only stood around outside waiting for their prey to come out."

"I have no idea. Never having been the object of a scandal before, I have no clue what the protocol is." Olivia paced the area between the couch and side chair.

"I thought maybe since you came from a wealthy family that you'd had media attention in the past."

"No." Olivia tried to smile at her friend's naivety. "Despite what you see on reality television, most people who have some assets aren't parading their lives to the world."

"Oh, so you weren't all over the papers when you lived up there?"

"No." Olivia shook her head. "My mother would have disowned me if I was in the papers. She lived by that old adage of a lady being in the paper three times in her life. At birth, when she married and then, technically, when she was dead, in her obituary."

The knocking at the door continued.

"You better see who that is," Sharon said.

"Open up. It's the sheriff."

"There's your answer." Olivia took a deep breath. Was she ready for this? To deal with that misogynist jerk again?

Knowing she had no choice, she stepped over to unlock and open the door.

As soon as she turned the knob, the wood was pushed toward her, and the bulky man shoved his way into her home.

The cacophony of voices from her yard caused Olivia to cringe. She took a second to peer out and noticed the man in the hand-tailored suit coming toward her with a companion. Bradford Roché. What the heck was Bradford doing here? Why surface now?

Before she could slam the door, he stepped onto the porch and pushed past her as well.

As he went by, he leaned over and tried to plant a

kiss on her cheek. Jerking her head back, Olivia made a hissing sound at him, hoping he'd take the hint and stop in his tracks.

No such luck. He settled on her couch, with only a small frown of distaste.

If she'd been in a better mood and her stomach wasn't in a state of total alarm at his being in her rented cabin, she might have laughed hysterically at what she knew had to be his total panic at being on a piece of furniture that had its best days in the 1960s. Or maybe the '70s.

"What's the purpose of all this?" Olivia waved her arm in the air to take in the sheriff, Roché, and the other man.

"It's my understanding, my dear, that this sheriff has some questions for you about the incident that occurred last evening. I've arranged for you to have the best legal counsel. He will be here for you during the interrogation and trial, if one is necessary."

"Thanks but no thanks. I have a lawyer already." Olivia thought she might actually cry again. She had to make one of the weirdest choices in her life. Allow the man they called a publicity hound to represent her or this stiff who was just like Bradford to do so. Somehow she knew she could trust the local man over the one her former fiancé brought around. He had to be one of his lapdogs. And how could she have missed Bradford for one second and cried over that song? It was obvious how pompous he was now that she'd been away from him for so long.

"I don't much care which one of the gents is your lawyer, missy. I just want your statement." The sheriff fiddled with his gun belt again. Olivia determined that must be a nervous mannerism. He seemed to do it a lot.

"Tell you what. Let me call Miguel Castro, and we'll come together to the station." She turned to Bradford. "Sorry you came such a long way. Be sure to have a good trip home." Returning to the front door, she opened it. "Now, I think it's time for me to take a shower and get ready for my day. It seems I have some company on my lawn. Maybe I'll start with making a statement to them."

She turned and strolled to her bathroom. Knowing Sharon was out in the living area and would be sure nothing untoward happened while Olivia herself was out of the room, she took a leisurely bath. The problem of when her mother's husband would show up or when he would send someone to try to harm her was foremost in her mind. She still needed to get away, but if she could get the media on her side, that might help.

Planning what to say while she washed her hair, Olivia soaped herself and hummed a song. Not the one that broke her heart. That was over.

Finally dressed for the day and feeling a bit as if she'd put on some armor along with her makeup, she left her bedroom and found Sharon alone and sitting on the couch looking at her cell phone.

"You got them to leave? Way to go."

"Yes, it seems they only wanted to talk to you." Sharon glanced up from the screen on her phone. "I guess I'm not particularly interesting."

Olivia nodded at Sharon's device. "But something on there definitely is."

"Is what?"

"Interesting. Aren't you paying attention to your own conversation?"

"I have to tell you, that Bradford Roché guy is definitely intriguing."

"Are you googling him?"

"Sure am." Sharon grinned. "He's handsome and apparently crazy-wealthy, but he's way too tightly wound. What did you ever see in him? I mean, look around us. You don't seem to be overly concerned with dollars. Anyone else would probably have put this landlord crap furniture in the basement and gotten something nicer to live with."

"You're right. I don't care about that stuff. I dated Bradford because my mother and his thought the idea was grand. To unite two good families would've made them both happy. At the time he dumped me, I thought I'd never get past it, and in fact, I cried over that stupid song just last night—God, was that only last night?—seems like forever ago now."

"Longest twenty-four hours of your life so far?" Sharon asked.

"Not the longest but it ranks up there in the top five."

"So you still miss this Bradford guy?" Sharon set her phone on the arm of the couch. "You said you were crying about him last night."

"Funny thing. I was bewailing the lost relationship less than a day ago, but as soon as he opened his mouth here in this silly little cabin that's been my refuge, I knew he'd been the brave one between us. By dumping me, he was doing me a huge favor. Just like his unbelievably expensive clothes didn't fit into the décor here, he doesn't really suit me or the life I want to live."

"Sounds to me as if the fiasco at the bar was actually a good thing since you can now move on from that heartache and maybe find someone more appropriate." She winked. "Maybe Rocky?"

"Right. No." Olivia laughed. "The mere fact that he's being kind at the moment is no reason to get carried away and think he might suit. He's too prickly for my taste."

"He'd probably say the exact thing about you."

"All the more reason to strike him off any list you're preparing in that little match-making head of yours."

Sharon looked coy. "I have no such list."

Olivia knew her friend's brain was going ninety miles an hour at the moment, picking out and discarding men she wanted to set her up with. It was almost a disease with her. Olivia was sorry Sharon couldn't seem to find someone for herself. She'd been successful with a lot of couples in town but never found lasting love in her own heart.

"By the way, Bradford—does he ever go by Brad?— said he wanted to take you to dinner tonight and asked me to give you his number so you could call him later."

"Not happening." Olivia shook her head. "What time am I meeting Miguel at the sheriff's office?"

Sharon glanced down at her watch. "Five minutes ago."

"My mother always said I liked to make an entrance." Olivia grabbed her purse. "Come on. Let's take your car. Maybe the reporters won't follow."

"Maybe the moon won't rise tonight."

"We can always hope, right?"

They left by the back door. Olivia, far from feeling as flippant as she was trying to sound to her friend, was apprehensive. What could they do to her? And, more importantly, if she were arrested and put in a holding cell, would it be open season on her life?

❧❧❧

Rocky tossed bales of hay off the back of the trailer he'd left them on too long. His leg had been bothering him, and he'd put off the job. This was what he needed at the moment, though. Some hard manual labor would take his mind off all that happened in the last day.

He was a little peeved—or more than a little—that he'd practically begged Olivia to allow him to help her. Why in the world would he want to get into another situation like he'd been in with Clara?

Clara. He let out a deep sigh. The woman he'd wanted to spend his life with. All those years ago. Before the military and before the injury. When he'd so arrogantly thought he could do anything, fix any problem. He'd learned differently. Much to his dismay.

Tossing more bales into the barn, he knew he'd pay the price later with the aching of his muscles and foot.

"Want some help?"

Glancing over his shoulder, Rocky spotted Sam leaning on the open door, dressed in neatly pressed slacks and wearing a long sleeve dress shirt. "I hardly think you're suitably attired for it."

"Wasn't talking about me."

"Then who? I don't see anyone else around."

"I meant I'd go and fetch someone." Sam laughed and stepped into the barn. "What's the demon on your back today? You're working as if the hounds of hell are your boss and said they'd throw you in a pit of starving boa constrictors if you don't get all that hay unloaded in the next two minutes."

"That's quite a vivid picture you paint there. And don't boas squeeze someone to death, not eat them?"

"They still eat their prey, they just don't chew."

"That's comforting."

"Seriously, what's bothering you?" Sam asked and held his hand out as if to help Rocky off the trailer.

"I got it, man." Rocky climbed off and set the pitchfork down. "I know I'll be aching soon, but I needed to get out some anger. What better way to do that than to work?"

"Who are you mad at?"

"Me."

"Kind of hard to make up with yourself, isn't it?"

"The hardest." Rocky shook his head to clear it. He needed to move on. Think of something else. "What brings you out here this morning?"

"I rode the motorcycle. Returning it. Do you have time to drive me home?"

"Sure. Let me go wash up, and I'll take you right in. You off work today?"

"No. I have a later shift on Mondays." Sam ran his hand through his hair. "I guess you saw all the news about Ollie." He paused then amended, "Olivia."

"I did. I went over to see if I could help her. That's why I'm mad at myself."

"Wait. What? Shouldn't you be mad at her if she turned you down?"

"Logically, yes, but I'm mad at my own arrogance. Who am I to think I can help her? She clearly has all the money and resources she needs to get herself the best lawyer in the state."

"She still needs her friends."

"Yeah, but do I even count in that number?" Rocky led the way out of the barn. He debated closing the doors but decided to leave them open since he didn't want to take the time to back the trailer out. Sam needed to get to town.

Inside the house, Rocky tugged his dirty shirt over his head and moved to the kitchen sink. Splashing warm water on his chest and face, he grabbed the dishwashing liquid and put some in his hand. Soaping up, he ran his palms over his neck and chest.

"I could've waited for you to take a shower, you know."

"No worries. I keep a stash of clean shirts down here. I don't need to change jeans since I'm going to be working some more once I return."

"You didn't need to change shirts just to drive me home."

"I was hoping we could get some lunch together at Myrna's. No one does chili like she does."

"You're right. The flavor is a bit different, and I'm not sure what she sneaks in there, but it's great. You've made me hungry now so hurry up."

Rocky reached around the corner of the propped-open swinging door that led into the dining room and grabbed a random T-shirt. He tugged it over his head then turned toward Sam. "Ready."

Sam laughed and moved his hand up and down to take in the shirt. "*Horton Hears a Who?* Really? That's *your* shirt?"

Rocky grinned. "Elephant and all."

"Did you pick it out yourself?"

"One of the kids I met at the hospital sent it last Christmas. I'm happy to wear it. That little guy almost died from injuries in a car accident. If he wants me in Horton, I'll wear Horton."

"You need a kid of your own. I got to see how great you were with them yesterday."

"I'm old fashioned enough to want the wife part first." Rocky snatched his keys from the countertop. "Come on. Myrna's chili waits for no man."

In the car, Sam said, "Can I ask you a question?"

"Sure. What do you want to know?"

"I couldn't help but notice the scarring on your back and arms. What happened?"

"Let's just say I was in the army and leave it at that."

"Okay. I won't pry, but if you ever want to talk, I'm good at keeping confidences."

"I appreciate it." Rocky drove on in silence and tried not to think about the torture he'd endured or the accident when the jeep ahead of his ran over that IED.

When they arrived at the diner, Rocky was surprised to see Olivia's former fiancé seated at a corner booth with another man. He had a look of scorn on his face as if the place were infected with bubonic plague.

Nothing made Rocky madder than someone being negative about his adopted town. He was tempted to go over and ask the man why he was in a restaurant he obviously felt was so beneath him. Only the fact that the man didn't know Rocky knew who he was stopped him from the confrontation.

"What's up your craw now?" Sam asked.

"Nothing. Why?" Rocky slid onto the bench seat at the closest booth.

Sam sat. "You're glaring at that city-slicker like you want to cut his head off his shoulders. What'd the man ever do to you?"

Leaning forward, Rocky whispered, "He's the former fiancé of Olivia."

"*What?*" The word was almost a squeal.

"Shush. He's right there."

"She was engaged? Man, she's a deep one. Full of secrets." Sam shook his head.

The door opened, and Russell walked in. Rocky, remembering Sam had a crush on him, called out, "Come on over and have some chili with us."

"Who is it?" Sam asked as his back was to the door. He glanced over his shoulder, whipped his head in Rocky's direction, and raised his eyebrows. A kick under the table let Rocky know even more than the panic on Sam's face that the man was torn between being excited to have Russell join them and scared he'd make a fool of himself in some way.

Russell slid in on the same side as Sam and smiled at them both. "Thanks for the invite. I don't really like to eat alone. I was going to sit at the counter and look friendless and sad."

"We saved you from all that," Sam said. "We're glad to have you. And truth be known, I hate to eat by myself, too."

A moment later, Olivia and Miguel Castro came in. Rocky cast a glance at her to try to warn her of the fiancé's presence, but it wasn't necessary as the man made himself known by striding across the small aisle between the booths and the counter stools.

"Olivia, we need to talk."

She backed up and almost collided with her lawyer. "No, we don't."

Turning around in the tiny space seemed to be difficult for her as she almost fell into the table in front of Rocky's. He wasn't in a position to help her, so he was glad to see Castro steady her by taking hold of her elbow.

"You can't avoid me forever," the fiancé said.

Rocky wished he could remember the man's name, but it was escaping him. Something fancy and pretentious but obviously forgettable.

"You have that wrong. I can." She was finally able to turn and placed her hand on Castro's upper arm. "Sorry, I need to cancel lunch. It seems I forgot a pressing appointment."

Castro stepped aside, and Olivia made a beeline for the exit. She was followed by the fiancé when he could get by Castro. Rocky almost laughed aloud at the sight of Castro and the man doing a cha-cha. He glanced up at Sam. "Mind if I bail on you and go after her?"

"What about being mad at yourself for trying to rescue her?"

"I've got more hay to unload so getting angry is useful."

"Go ahead then. I'll catch a cab home after Russell and I eat."

"No worries. I'll take you home," were the last words Rocky heard from Russell as he ran out of the café himself. Well, limped quickly. The pain had kicked in from his efforts earlier.

As he lumbered up the street, he couldn't help but be glad that Sam and Russell were going to have some time to get to know each other better. It was one good thing about the day.

He caught up to Olivia and the fiancé in the park. At the edge of it. She stood on the grass as if ready to make a dash for it, and the fiancé was next to a bench.

Rocky sauntered up and did something he knew he might regret as she would probably smack him. Placing his arm around her, he kissed her lightly on the mouth.

Before she could react, he said, "Darling, you ran out

of the diner so fast, I didn't know what happened." He nodded at the fiancé. "Is this man bothering you?"

To his surprise, Olivia played along. "This is my former fiancé. You remember, I told you about him. The one I was so glad to escape because that breakup led me to you."

"*Escape?* You know you were devastated when I left. All your friends told me so when you disappeared. We all thought you'd killed yourself." The arrogant twit was actually arguing with his former fianceé about how much *she* loved him when he was the louse who left her? Unbelievable.

"Sir, I don't know you, but believe me when I say this gorgeous woman would never be suicidal over a man." The irony of the situation did not escape Rocky's notice. Clara was one who would commit suicide. He still blamed himself for that every day of his life.

"Why won't you sit down with me and discuss our future?" the man asked Olivia.

"Because we don't have a future." With Rocky's arm still around her waist, Olivia said, "Please understand. The best thing you did for me was break it off. We both know we were only together because our mothers wanted it for the families. You don't love me, and I don't love you."

"I realized about a month after we broke up that I *do* love you, and I wanted to come back. And now you're telling me you want a future with some scarred clown who dresses in a cartoon T-shirt, ratty jeans, and scuffed cowboy boots? Please. I'm not an idiot, you know. The debutante of the year doesn't change *that* much."

"But you didn't come back, did you? And I'll thank you not to insult my boyfriend." Olivia leaned into Rocky. Her body shook as it rested on his side. He couldn't tell if she was scared or angry. She had a weird smile pasted on her face.

"You're right. I didn't come back. I'm sorry to say I didn't know how to make it up to you."

"If you really loved me, you'd have found a way. I have to wonder why you're here now—" She held her hand up to keep him from speaking. "—don't get me wrong. I don't *care,* but I do wonder why you would show up."

"Because you've been found, and I love you? Isn't that good enough?"

"No." She shook her head. "And I haven't been found. I wasn't lost." She turned to Rocky. "Let's go, Graham. I think I want to celebrate being released by the sheriff by making love all afternoon. After all—" She looked at her watch. "—it's been about six hours since our last orgasms."

"Right you are." Rocky barely kept himself from laughing at her words. He kissed her lightly again then turned to the fiancé. "Sorry you blew it with her but, really, thanks for doing that so I could have her."

He led Olivia away and toward his truck.

When they were out of earshot, he said, "Bravo. I don't know what happened with the two of you, but you handled that encounter better than I think a lot of women would have."

"Thanks. I somehow don't think I've seen the last of him. I *do* appreciate your help there and don't think I don't remember I owe you an apology for this morning."

"You don't owe me anything. I enjoyed what just happened. It really made my day." He took hold of her hand. "To tell the truth, the rest of the day could only get better if I was really going to get to make love the rest of the afternoon."

She laughed. "Any particular lady in mind or just any old girl will do?"

"I plead the fifth on that." Rocky wouldn't have said last week that he wanted to make love with Olivia, but in the previous thirty or so hours, things seemed to have changed. "By the way, I'm holding your hand in case old stiff-neck is still watching us."

"Old Stiff-Neck sounds like the perfect name for him. It's a wonder I didn't see it when we were dating."

"Love sometimes blinds us to such things."

"I'm not sure I ever really loved him. What about you? Have you ever been in love?" Olivia asked the question as they reached his truck.

Rocky opened the passenger door for her, not wanting to discuss Clara and the wounds that would open for him.

"No. Can't say that I have." He crossed his fingers behind his back, not that he was superstitious. Nope, not at all.

"Then we're a pair then."

"Why agree to marry someone who you didn't love? In this day and age?"

Olivia got in the truck. Before he closed the door, she gave him a sad smile. "Beats the hell out of me. I guess I was doing what my mother wanted. One tends to obey her or suffer the consequences."

"And what were the consequences of the breakup?"

"She lapsed into a coma before she learned about it. I guess when, or if, she wakes up, I'll have to explain why. Something for another day, right?"

"Right," he said and closed the door.

Walking around to his side of the vehicle, he shot a glance in the direction of the park. The former fiancé was still standing where they left him, watching as if his life depended on it.

Rocky's antenna went up. His instincts when he was army intelligence were honed and quite good. He trusted them now. This guy was up to something, and it wasn't wooing an old flame. No indeed.

Chapter 7

Olivia could barely fathom what had happened. The session with the sheriff went better than she anticipated. Her lawyer was actually pretty competent, and he handled the good old boys as if he took them down every day.

Since there would be no criminal charges, she was free to go. Leave town.

Taking her lawyer out to lunch was the least she could do before vanishing. She'd almost had a coronary when she saw Bradford in the diner. It stunned her to see him there. It was completely out of the realm of possibilities that the man would deign to eat in such an establishment.

Now here she was in Graham Rockford's truck being driven back to her house. How in the world that happened, she was still sorting out. The whole experience in the park was also surreal.

"What world issue are you planning to solve?" Graham asked.

"Huh? What?"

"You've got some deep thought going on there. I was asking what about."

"Mulling over the last day and a half and trying to wrap my head around how we got here."

"It's been a roller coaster for sure."

"I know. And I still need to get to the bank."

"I'll take you right now. We're right down the street. Not that I'm in a hurry to see you leave town but I get that you need to go."

"I'm with you. I don't really *want* to leave, but I don't have a choice. Now that it's known where I am, I'm not safe."

Rocky pulled into a parking spot near the bank. Before she got out, he said, "Not that I'm in the habit of accusing everyone I meet of criminal motives, but is there any way the former fiancé could be working with your mother's husband?"

"Bradford in cahoots with that evil man?" She sat for a minute, processing that idea. Finally, she said, "I'm not sure. They didn't ever seem that close, but I'm not willing to rule it out. After all, Bradford *did* show up here, and I know it's not because he loves me. There has to be *some* motive."

"Until we know, I hope you won't go anywhere alone."

"I won't. Besides—" She sent him a small smile. "—I'll be gone before he gets another chance to corner me."

He opened his door. "To be sure of that, let me escort you into the bank."

"No argument here. Thanks. Especially, after how horrible I was to you this morning."

"Forget that. You were under stress. Still are, for that matter." Graham stepped out of the truck.

Olivia noticed him wince as his foot touched the ground.

"Are you all right?"

"Yes. Old injury. It flares up once in a while."

"Do you need help?"

"No. I'm used to it. Come on, let's get your business taken care of so you can get out of here."

She stopped in her tracks and stood at the back of the truck.

"What?" he asked.

"This morning, you wanted me to hide out at your place and not run off, and now you seem to be so eager to get rid of me that you're practically willing to pack my bags for me."

"Like I already said, it's not that I *want* you to leave, it's just now that I've seen your former fiancé and noticed how intently he was watching us, I'm afraid he may be a source of danger for you as well."

"What? You think he's here to harm me?"

"That's why I asked if he and your mother's husband were friends. Maybe this Bradford was sent here to scope out the lay of the land before they made a move."

She shuddered. *Good grief. This is not good.* But wait a second. Why should she believe it was true merely because this man said it might be? Who was he?

"I don't think that's right, but one thing I *do* agree

with is I need to get my business conducted so I can make my way out of this mess." Olivia walked past the truck and stepped on the curb to make her way down the sidewalk to the bank. She could hear Graham behind her. His boot dragged the concrete once in a while and made her feel sorry for him. She'd never known he had any kind of issue with his leg and wondered what caused it and why it was flaring up now.

Inside the bank, she approached the desk to sign in to gain access to her safe deposit box. After checking her ID, even though he knew her, the manager took the bank's key from a locked drawer and led her toward the vault where the room to view the boxes was.

The manager made short work of his part of unlocking the box. Once she inserted her own key and the manager pulled the metal box from its space in the wall, he left her alone.

Opening the lid, a tear escaped as soon as she saw the photo placed on top. She didn't remember doing that, but she must have. The sight of her father's smiling face staring up at her made her sad but gave her courage at the same time. Maybe her subconscious knew she'd need that little bit of encouragement the next time she came to this box.

Gathering all the items inside without really looking at them since she didn't plan to return, Olivia shoved them into her bag. She'd leave the box available since she'd paid a year in advance, but she didn't expect to see this place again.

Another stray tear fell. She wiped her face and stood

up straight. *No time to be maudlin. Buck up and move on. It's not like it's the first time I've had to pull out.* Of course, somehow, this time, she'd left her heart unguarded and fell in love with the town and the people who were in her life as well as that country bar she never thought she'd get attached to. This was, by far, the hardest move. Except for that first one. When her mother initially fell into the coma, and Olivia realized she was next.

That was more of a panicked flight. And while she'd been a bit frantic last night, the more the day went on, and she was still here, the more Olivia let herself relax. And trust she would be fine.

She let out a bark of a laugh. No, she wouldn't be fine. Unless she hid again. This time for good. No more making friends. She could do it. Be a loner for a year and ten months. How hard could it be?

Coming out of the room, she nodded to the manager. "Thanks. All done. I put the box back in its slot."

"Thank you, Miss Jacobs. We'll see you again soon."

She smiled and waved, too choked up to answer.

Nodding at Graham, she walked out of the bank, knowing he would follow. He was, even after all the bickering they'd been through during the time she'd lived in town, a loyal friend. He'd proven that in the last day or so.

In his truck, she turned, leaned on her left hip and looked over at him. "Thank you."

He inserted his key and cranked the engine. "For what?"

"Everything. I know I've been acting like an ungrateful wretch, but I really am thankful for all your help."

"No worries. I know." He backed out of the parking space and headed down Main Street.

Soon they were on the highway and headed for her little rented cabin. An arrow of pain pierced her heart. She really would miss that place. Ratty sofa and Formica dinette and everything.

A black car came up beside them.

"What the heck? Watch out, Graham, that lunatic is trying to pass on this narrow road. What's he thinking?"

As if to answer her question, the car came over and rammed the side of Graham's truck.

"He's trying to kill us," Olivia screamed.

"Maybe he's just a bad driver and thought he was past us and could move over."

She noticed Graham's fingers were white as he gripped the steering wheel and, even though his words were said calmly, she could tell he didn't believe them.

"Bull, Graham. That person is after us. I know it."

The black car rammed them again.

"He's trying to run us off the road for sure," she cried out.

"I see that now. Twice can't be an accident. Hold on. I'm going to lose this guy."

Graham hit the gas. The truck fishtailed. Holding back her scream, Olivia grabbed hold of the hand rest and held on with all her might.

This was going to get crazier. Graham was driving like a man possessed and so was the guy in the black car.

She tried to see who was in that vehicle but the windows were tinted too dark. Great. They wouldn't even be able to identify the person if they survived this.

"Where are we going?" Olivia called out.

"Doesn't matter right now. I'm going to shake him off, and then we can decide what to do."

Making an internal decision to keep her mouth shut so he could concentrate, Olivia stopped asking questions. That didn't mean they weren't still rolling around in her head. It was clear she wasn't going to be able to go back to the cabin now.

They jockeyed back and forth with the black car ramming them over and over. Olivia wondered how the front end of the vehicle and Graham's door were staying intact. The bumps got progressively more violent as they went.

Some of the trees on her side of the road got a little too close for comfort as the truck ran along the shoulder occasionally.

The rocks and dirt spurted up along their path. At least Graham had some kind of training or skill that he was drawing on to keep them on the pavement.

Just as that thought sped through her mind, the truck went off the road. The bumps were incredible. She hit her head on the roof several times, jarring her teeth and even making her bite her tongue. "Ouch."

"Tough, isn't it?" Graham glanced quickly in her direction then back at the path they were cutting through the terrain. At least the few trees that had been in their way earlier had thinned out to nothing.

"Most turbulent flight I've ever had."

"That's nothing. Watch this." He threw the truck into neutral and turned the steering wheel. They fishtailed wildly.

Because the black car was right beside them, the rear of the truck smacked it as it rotated.

The driver of that vehicle didn't have the skills Graham did. The car careened out of control and flipped over several times.

Olivia covered her eyes. She didn't want to see what happened next.

She needn't have worried. As soon as they were straight and headed back in the other direction, Graham slammed his foot on the accelerator and put some distance between them and the overturned car.

"Do you think he's all right?" she asked.

"Do you really care? If he is, he gets another shot at taking you out, doesn't he?"

"If you put it that way, then no. I guess I was feeling some sympathy for a fellow human being in danger."

Graham shook his head. "Leave it to you to get all sappy about the person trying to kill you." He paused for a second as he took a turn at a hair-raising speed. "And me, in the process."

"By the way, what kind of engine do you have in this thing? I've been around cars my whole life, and I've never seen a Chevy move like this one did back there."

"Never mind. Let's just say I do some tinkering myself."

"Yeah. Some kind of tinkering there, mister. You've saved our lives and, even though I'm not happy about having to hide out for two more years, I *am* happy about still being alive to do so."

"I don't think it's safe to go back to your place. By now, if that dude back there survived that flip, he's called someone, and they know where we are and what vehicle we're in."

"So what do we do?"

"Head to my ranch and get one of my other automobiles. I'll also need to find someone to take care of the livestock while I'm gone getting you somewhere safe."

"No. I can't ask you to do that. Just get me to the closest airport, and I'll get a ticket under my fake passport and make myself scarce."

"Since you have no luggage, I think you probably don't have that passport on you. Unless you had another one in the safe deposit box."

"Damn. You're right. Maybe Sharon can get my bag and get it to your ranch."

"No. Not a chance. You don't want her in danger, do you?"

"Of course not." A chill ran down Olivia's spine. "Would they really harm her?"

"Based on my experience, they would probably grab her to use as bait to lure you out. Hell, they might anyway, once they learn of your connection."

"I sure hope not. And while we're chatting about your *experience*, where did you learn to drive like that?"

"Tactical skills school." The truck roared on toward his place, she presumed. She'd never been there, so she wasn't exactly sure where he lived.

"Where does one sign up for such a thing?" she asked.

"One must first sign up for military service."

"Oh, yeah. I think I heard you used to be in the service. What branch?"

"Army." The terse tone of his responses clued her in on the fact he didn't want to discuss that time in his life.

He turned in on a dirt road almost obscured by low vegetation. "This is the start of my land."

"How many acres?"

"Three hundred and fifty."

A thought occurred to her. "Wait a second. How do we know the man who was running us off the road or the people he was working with didn't find out where you live? Couldn't they be waiting for us here? Why is this a good idea?"

"Because I have them outsmarted." Graham tossed her a grin that would have been sexy if she hadn't been so scared. Who knew how cute he could be?

"What do you mean?"

"We're not going to my actual house. We're going to another building on the property."

"And that will help us how?"

"It's all about secret passageways and hidden rooms."

∞∞∞

When they arrived at the guesthouse on the ranch, Rocky said, "We'll get out here, and once I check to see that we're alone, I'll take the truck and park it in a place to throw them off."

"How will you get back? Don't think I don't remember your foot or leg is hurting. You can't walk a long way."

"You just stay hidden, and I'll return before you know it. I can walk as far as I need to." He didn't want to admit to her that she was right about the pain in his leg. It had already been hurting before the car chase. Now that he'd been jostled along and rammed on the same side as the bad leg, he wasn't sure at all he could go on. But he had to.

Rocky knew he could dig deep when he needed to and this would be one of those occasions. He had to get the truck away from the house. Otherwise, it would lead Olivia's stalkers right to them.

He parked and tried to make sure as he got out that she couldn't tell he was in more pain than before.

No such luck.

"You really can't manage this. Let me drive the truck and park it. I can get back here faster," she said.

"We have to make sure you're safe. It may take me a while, but you'll be okay here alone."

"I'm not comfortable about this."

He unlocked the door. "I know, but I'll be safer out there than you will. They don't really want me."

"But you said they could use Sharon as a lure to bring me out. What about you? Couldn't the same thing happen?"

"Hardly. If they caught me, they wouldn't be able to

get anything out of me about where you are, and if they ask around, they'll hear we don't really get along, right?"

"Except you and I both indicated to Bradford that we're in a relationship, and you think he's part of all this."

"News flash. He didn't believe one word of that crap." Rocky laughed. "Come on in and let me get you settled."

They stepped inside. She let out a gasp. "Oh, Graham, what a lovely house."

"Thanks. It's very old. I had it moved here."

"Really?"

"Yeah. It was my grandmother's place. I wanted to preserve it." He led her into the paneled dining room.

"Where am I going to hide?"

Moving over to the fireplace, Rocky reached for the secret button near one end of the mantel. The paneling moved, exposing a narrow passageway.

"Wow." Olivia peered into the opening. "It's tight in there."

"It is but at the top is a nice room where you'll be safe. Come on. You go first, and I'll close it as we go up. There are seven stairs then a sharp turn to get past the chimney. Then six more steps to the room."

Olivia went on and let out a little squeal as she squeezed past the turn.

He took his time, nursing the leg a bit.

When he stepped into the room, she was standing in the middle of the space. "This is nice. I'm glad to see there are some books. Maybe I can read while I wait."

She smiled ruefully. "If I can quit worrying long enough."

"No need to worry. You'll be as safe here as if you lived in a safe deposit box yourself."

She glanced around. "This is kind of the same thing, isn't it?"

"I think so." He gave a small bow. "And now, milady, I go." He returned to the staircase.

Before he stepped down, Olivia said, "For the record, when I said I wanted to stop worrying, I mean about you being out there and in pain."

Stunned at her words, he couldn't find his voice to comment. Instead, he turned and blew her a kiss. When he *could* speak, he said, "Thank you," then made his way out down and out of the house.

Taking time to stop in the kitchen, even though he knew he needed to be on the move, Rocky grabbed a bottle of ibuprofen. He shook out a handful and shoved them into his mouth, wishing he had something stronger.

Limping more than he wanted, he made his way to the truck and thought about where to take it. He didn't want to go too far, but he wanted to be sure it wouldn't lead to them. His initial plan to get his other vehicle had changed.

It was obvious they knew his name, and if they had access to trace his tags, they'd learn what automobile he and Olivia were in. Since anyone could search the ownership records of cars online, it was only a matter of confirming the tag on the make and model of the auto they were seeking.

Trying to decide who it would be safe to borrow a ride from, Rocky discarded everyone he thought about. If the aggressive driving recurred, he'd be asking a friend to sacrifice their car to the accident gods. That wouldn't be fair.

The sun was well on its way to setting now. Finding a dark area in the middle of his acreage was easy. He pulled the truck into a thicket of underbrush and trees and got out.

In his haste to get on the trek back to the house, he landed wrong on the bad leg. Sucking in a hiss of pain, he sat on the running board for a moment to catch his breath. Blasted injury.

Then Rocky checked himself. Plenty of the men in those jeeps that day would've traded him the broken leg over the loss of their lives. He knew he was lucky, just some days he let it get the best of him.

This was no time to wallow in pain or pity. He needed to move.

Now that it was almost fully dark, it would be more difficult maneuvering on the rocky terrain. Lots of bigger rocks mixed in with the dirt, grass and smaller stones would make it easier for him to go down before he knew it.

Eventually, as he walked along, his eyes adjusted enough for him to make good headway. He stopped once in a while to rub his calf muscle but, all in all, Rocky was pleased with the progress he made.

Until he saw the headlights in the distance. Coming from the direction of his grandmother's house. As if whoever was in the vehicle had already been there and done whatever damage they intended.

Breaking into a loping run, dragging his left leg through the dirt, Rocky prayed as he went. Daring to hope Olivia had stayed put and not ventured out of the secret room, he kept up a brutal pace until he got within a hundred yards of the house.

Falling to his belly, he crept along, looking for signs that whoever was in the car he'd seen was either gone or had never been there. He didn't think whoever it was had been randomly on his property. It wasn't like this was a well-beaten path.

He spied some tire tracks in the drive at the front of the house. Torn between making a move to go inside to check on Olivia or sitting out here watching for anyone left behind to keep an eye on the place, Rocky decided to err on the side of caution and keep where he was for a while.

The severe cramping in his leg helped make his decision. It would be a few minutes before it would quit spasming anyway.

Ever alert, even through the pain, he lay there on his belly for what seemed forever. The only thing he saw move was a doe and her two fawns.

Finally deciding it was safe to venture inside, he crawled on his stomach until he reached the back porch. Using the bottom of the handrail to the steps leading up, he was able to get to his feet.

Once he was erect, praying the wood deck wouldn't creak, Rocky moved to the door and put his ear against the glass pane in the upper half. Listening intently, he stood where he was and counted off a full five minutes.

Hearing no signs of life, he inserted his key and found the door actually wasn't locked. Digging deep into his memory banks, he tried to remember if he checked it before he left earlier. He and Olivia had used the front door.

Not sure about when he last used that door, and if he'd assumed it was locked when he went to hide the truck, Rocky took a chance and opened the door.

No one jumped out to grab him, so he moved on into the kitchen. His heart fell to his knees. The place was ransacked.

Moving stealthily to the corner cabinet, Rocky opened it quietly and reached for one of the six cereal boxes on the shelf. The Cocoa Puffs held a Glock.

Digging his hand in, the cold metal feel of the weapon gave him some solace. The scumbags may have torn up his furniture—why, he didn't know, since, clearly, the kitchen table didn't hide their prey—but now he was more than ready for them. Let one of the jackasses still be in his house. If they were, they were going down. Hard.

Creeping around the corner to the living area, he did a quick scan. No one. Clearing the next room, he did the same, and finally ended up in the room with the secret passage. He tapped the button at the mantel, and the door slid open. Easing himself inside, he closed the panel as quickly as he could, just in case.

Tired, wiped out really, he didn't know if he could muster the energy to make it up the stairs.

Worried about Olivia, he knew he had to get to her. Drawing in a deep breath, he took the first step. Counting as he went and knowing how many were left seemed to help spur him on.

At the top, he collapsed into the room. It was as if his body finally gave out on him. Barely able to comprehend what he saw, he shook his head to help him focus.

Chapter 8

Olivia held the only weapon she could find. Well, one she'd made. When she heard the men downstairs tearing up the place obviously looking for her with malice in their hearts, she'd first cowered in the corner and tried not to cry out in panic.

When they were directly below, she could hear their voices—she couldn't make out exactly what was said as it was too muffled by the chimney—but they were clearly angry not to find anyone in the house.

Convinced they would find the secret passage and be on her at any moment, she'd taken advantage of the sounds from below. Taking a chance they would think the noise she made was merely part of their own handiwork, she broke off a leg from one of the chairs in the room.

The wood splintered nicely. Jutting pieces of broken wood would inflict some damage if she had to use it to whack someone. She was under no illusions that the piece of wood could actually save her life but she wasn't going down without a fight.

Once she had her weapon, Olivia stood by the door leading to the hidden staircase with it upraised. The element of surprise was on her side.

After a time, her arm grew sore, so she let it down but didn't relax her guard.

Eventually, it got quiet downstairs, and she thought she heard a car start.

Hopeful they were gone, she sat where she was and let out a breath she didn't know she was holding.

Once it got quiet, thoughts and worries crept in. Hours had to have passed. What had become of Graham? Olivia glanced around the room for a clock to see what time it was. None.

Who had a room with no clock? She shook her head. She'd stopped wearing a watch when she left home. Her favorite one was from her father but it was a Rolex, and she needed to make sure she looked the part of a non-wealthy woman. She hadn't been able to bring herself to wear any other.

Now she regretted it. How long *had* he been gone?

She stood and paced, keeping her makeshift weapon at her side, torn about what to do. Graham told her to stay hidden. But if he was hurt and needed her, shouldn't she go to him? After all he'd done for her, it was the least she could do.

In the moment she decided she couldn't stay still any longer, she heard a noise.

Craning her neck, she listened more intently than she ever had before. When she recognized the sound, her heart stilled.

Tiptoeing to the stairs, she stood to the side, ready to clobber whoever came up them and opened that door.

When it swung into the room, she made her move. Holding the chair leg over her head, she slashed it through the air.

In the split second she recognized Graham, she tossed the weapon aside and fell to her knees beside him. "Oh my God, you look awful."

He glanced up and gave her a lopsided, exhausted grin. "That's the nicest thing anyone has said to me all day." He cast a sidelong look at the discarded bat she'd made. "And thanks for not knocking my head in with that."

"I've been frantic with worry. I was sure they would find one of us. Either you outside or me in here. When you opened the secret panel, I was afraid it was them again." Olivia took a deep, shuddering breath. "They were here earlier."

"Yeah. I saw that. They made a right mess down there. Why they did that, I don't know. The crazy thing is, there was no way a human woman could be hiding in a kitchen table, but they destroyed it as well as all the china in the china cabinet."

"Oh no. I'm so sorry. You've lost your grandmother's china because of me." Of all the things that had happened this day, that was the one that sent Olivia over the edge. She burst into tears.

"Wait. Stop." Graham sat up and took her hand.

She wiped her eyes. "What?"

"I got that china at a flea market. My sister has Grandmom's china."

"Oh, thank goodness. I'm so glad."

"Well, that stuff *did* set me back a few hundred bucks." He winked.

"I've got a wad of cash in my bag. I'll pay you back."

"No need. I was teasing."

"Come in and sit down. Do you think it's safe to go down to the kitchen and get you something to drink? You looked wiped out."

"I *am* wiped out. And I wouldn't suggest we go down just yet."

He moved as if to rise. When he tried to pull his left leg into a standing position, it seemed to give out.

Olivia moved as fast as she could to put her shoulder under his armpit to help him.

Once he was on his feet, she was stunned to find he could barely move.

She assisted him to the closest chair, an overstuffed, rolled arm thing.

Graham eased into it and let out a sigh. "Sorry. This is the most action I've seen in a very long while. I'm not used to it anymore."

"I still think I need to go down and get you some water or something. You have no idea how pale and washed out your face is."

"I think I probably do. I've been nursing this thing for a long time. There's a half-bathroom up here if I needed water but I think I'd rather have a shot or three of whiskey."

"Of course I remember there's a bathroom up here. I've used it while you were gone." Olivia laughed, shocked at how nervous she sounded talking about using the facilities with him. Gee. Everyone had bodily functions. Why was she being so weird about it?

"Did you happen to look inside that globe over there?" He tilted his head toward the far corner of the room.

"Nope. I've never looked *into* any globe. I thought all they had to offer was on the outside."

"*Au contraire*, inside that globe there is the nectar of the gods. You've been missing out. Poor sheltered one that you are."

She darted a look at him to see if he was serious about the sheltered comment but was glad she didn't overreact when she saw the smile on his face. He didn't even seem to realize what he said could've been interpreted another way. A slur on her being a rich socialite.

Then it dawned on her. He didn't think of her that way at all. In his mind, she was a woman who owned a country bar. Not sure if she liked that characterization, she moved over to the globe, hoping the redness she could sense on her face wasn't showing.

When she reached the globe, she could tell the center section lifted. Pulling up on it, she laughed when she saw the contents. A full bar. Complete with low-ball glasses.

"What's your pleasure? There are two different whiskies over here."

"The Scottish single malt, please. The other was a bottle my sister liked. An old Kentucky one."

"So you're a true Scotch man?" She poured a couple fingers for him and carried it over.

Noting that his hand shook as she gave it to him, Olivia said, "Let me help you take off those boots. I bet you'd feel better if your feet could breath."

"Feet can breathe?" He grinned then gulped down the shot.

"You know what I mean."

"I think I need another drink." Graham held the cut-crystal glass out. It wasn't Baccarat, but it was a nice set.

"Are you using the whiskey to self-medicate?"

"Yes. It helps when there aren't any pain pills to hand."

"My dad always said pain pills don't help. They just make it where you don't care that you're hurting."

"Your dad was a wise man. He was absolutely right." He waggled his glass. "I need some more 'don't care' medicine."

She shook her head but refilled his glass anyway since they weren't going anywhere any time soon. If ever.

That sobered her. What *were* they going to do?

"What just happened?" Graham asked.

"Nothing. Why?"

"You had a look on your face as if you were about to panic."

"I was, but that's for tomorrow. Tonight, we need to get your boots off. I don't want to have to cut them off if your feet are swollen like I think they probably are."

"We're safe up here for now, and I'm going to find a way to get you clear of this threat hanging over you." He handed her the now empty glass. "I'm ashamed to say I *will* need some help with my boots. I don't think I can bend that far right now."

Olivia set the whiskey on the side table and knelt by Graham's feet.

She tugged on the right one first. It was easier than she thought and he didn't even flinch. Taking that as a good sign, Olivia grabbed hold of his left foot at the heel and pulled on the boot.

He hissed through his teeth.

Glancing up at his face, she was stunned to see the grimace of sheer agony on it. "I'm so sorry. I thought the other one came off so easily that this one would as well."

"That's my bad leg."

"Oh, yes. I remember you saying that you had a bad leg. You don't often favor it, so I forgot."

"Do you want me to try to get it off myself?"

"No, no. I want to help. It's the least I can do. I'll be gentle." Olivia took her time and slowly eased the boot first from his heel and then all the way off. She kept a close eye on his face while she worked. She didn't want to hurt him any more than she already had.

When it was off, at last, she touched his foot softly. "I think we need to take the sock off. It could be con-stricting the blood flow."

"I haven't had a pedicure lately so don't let my toes scare you."

He was trying to joke with her, but she could tell by the paleness of his face and the dark rings under his eyes that he really was about to pass out.

"Let's get another dose of medicine down you." She stood and refilled the glass. With a lot more then she'd previously given him. The size of his foot scared her. It was massive. Had he reinjured it? In the name of saving her?

Graham took the offered whiskey and, as she removed the sock from his foot, he took another long drink.

When the foot was bare, it was all Olivia could do not to cry. How in the world did the man function with such a limb? How did he keep his secret?

"Looks pretty grim, doesn't it?"

"I can't believe you don't have a limp all the time." She sat on her bottom and gently rubbed his foot, hoping to bring some relief to him.

"I do when I don't have on boots or shoes. If you notice, one is built up more than the other. It evens my stride."

"That's pretty clever."

"I have to say, it wasn't my idea, but I'm grateful to the doctor who suggested it."

"Were you injured in the army?"

"Yeah. But I've adapted as you can tell." He made a face. "Unless and until I overdo it like I did today."

"For me."

He nodded. "Yes. For you. And I would do it again." He put his hand on the top of her head. "Any time."

"Thanks. I don't know why. I've been a wretch to you over the last couple of years, but you came right to the rescue." What she said reminded her of what he'd said when he left her and Sharon at her house. Good God. Had that been just this morning? What a long day it had turned out to be.

"It was all in good fun, right? Banter?"

"If that's the way you choose to recall it, then I'll take that. It puts me in a better light anyway." She took a chance. "May I ask you a question?"

"What's that?"

"When you left my house after I rejected your offer to help this morning, you said something about having a hero complex. I was wondering what you meant by that comment."

"Let's just say I tend to jump in where I'm not wanted and leave it at that." The previously open look on his face seemed to close down, letting her know she'd touched a sore spot. Maybe sorer than his poor foot. Better to let it go.

"I'm sorry if I stepped on your toes, either just now or this morning when I was acting ungrateful for your offer. I can't help but think I might be dead right this moment if not for you."

"No need to get melodramatic." He smiled, seeming more comfortable now that she'd let go of the obviously touchy subject.

"It's true. I'm not exaggerating."

"I'm sorry for the accommodations up here. I can't offer you a hot meal, but I do have some granola bars stashed away in the book case if you want a snack before turning in."

"I'd love a nibble of something. I missed lunch as you know."

"You definitely made haste to leave Myrna's when you spotted Bradford."

Graham exaggerated the pronunciation of Bradford's name in such a way as to make her former fiancé sound as completely snobbish as he was.

Olivia laughed then said, "Wait."

"What is it?"

"You just said a snack before I turned in." She glanced around the room. "Turn in where? I see no bed here, and I presume it's not safe to go downstairs if we plan to sleep since we could easily be discovered."

"That's another surprise."

"What? Where you stash the bed?"

"Let's just say this house is full of mystery."

⌒⌒⌒

Even though he felt like dying and never moving again, Rocky got a kick out of the look on Olivia's face when he hinted he kept a bed hidden in the room. That there actually *was* a Murphy bed in the space didn't do anything to abate his humor about it.

He really needed to get out of his jeans. They seemed to be constricting his legs more and more the longer he had them on. How to tell Olivia he needed to strip down to his boxers was the question foremost in his mind.

"Where are we going to sleep? I don't see that chair as being comfortable for you. You need to stretch out your leg, and the floor isn't all that either." She stood and rubbed her rear. "My tush is already sore from these few moments down there."

"Have you ever heard of a Murphy bed?"

"Sure. Isn't that one of the things they used to have in the 1960s? It came out of the wall?"

Rocky nodded. "Yep. Would you believe it if I told you there was one up here?"

"Nothing would surprise me now."

"Over there then." He pointed to the far wall, next to the bookcase. "If you move that small table there and put it in front of the bookshelf, you'll find the handle for the bed there. Pull it toward you and then you'll see."

She moved the table and soon had the bed down. There was a set of sheets folded neatly at the end when she had it open. "Oh good," she said, "I was worried for a second."

"About us having to sleep together?" He grinned but was really afraid of what she would say to that. He'd been wondering how long it would take her to realize the meaning of there only being one bed in the room. Much as he would like to do the honorable thing and take the floor, he knew he'd never make it through the night on that hard surface. It was all he could do to hold it together in the chair.

"Nonsense. That's a given. One bed, two people. I'm no math genius, but I worked that out." She laughed. "I was more concerned that there would be old, dusty sheets on the bed." Turning to face him, she added, "And now you know my deepest secret. I have to have clean sheets."

"If that's the worst thing about you, I can handle it." He snapped his fingers. "Wait. Do you snore?"

"You'll have to wait and see." She set to work getting the bed ready.

"There's a blanket in the chest along this wall." Rocky really needed to get out of his jeans. "I'm going to try to make it to the bathroom to get out of these pants. I hope you don't mind my boxers." It pained him mentally to add, "It feels like I'm losing circulation in my lower extremities."

"Oh, good God. Come on. I'm not a prim little virgin. Let me help you." She strode across the room to stand beside him. Helping him to stand, she put her shoulder under his arm and hoisted him up. "Unzip yourself."

He hated this. Being almost helpless in front of a woman was not something he relished, but right now, he had no choice but to have her assist him. Dead on his feet and half-drunk with the whiskey as well as the pain, he unfastened his pants and was able to slide them down his thighs. Once they were at that level, Rocky had to be seated to get them the rest of the way off. The right leg was easy. When he couldn't get the denim fabric past his swollen calf, he sat in silence for a moment.

Frustration welled in him. Now he looked like a fool. One leg on and one leg off. How humiliating.

Olivia stared at him. Not with pity. Or at least he hoped not.

"Where are the scissors? Tell me you have some up here."

"I don't know. My sister used to come up and sew some when she was around. Maybe in the little tote bag she kept stashed up here. Over on the bookcase. It's blue and gold with some kind of swirly design."

Olivia made her way back to the bookcase and came back with a small pair of scissors. She held them up. "These are tiny but hopefully can cut through that thick fabric. Or at least get me started so I can rip them off you."

To cover his embarrassment, he said, "Can I pass the word all over town that you got me in a double bed and tore my jeans off me?"

"I haven't gotten you into bed yet, so save the story for now." She knelt in front of him for about the fifth time that evening.

In a few moments, she had his pants off and waved them around. "Say goodbye to these."

Then she glanced at his leg. He braced himself for the questions, but they didn't come. She merely held her hand out, "Do you need help getting over to the bed?"

"No. I can do it. Need to make a trip to the bathroom first."

"Before you go, where's the stash of granola bars? I think we both need one or two."

"Can't eat in bed. The clean sheet rule, you know."

"Yes, I *do* know. It's my rule, remember?"

"Granola over there." He pointed to the bookcase again. "Fourth shelf behind *War and Peace.*"

"Weird choice."

"Not really. When you think about it, it fits." He limped toward the bathroom.

"How so?"

Over his shoulder, he said, "When you're hungry, your stomach is fighting with you. Once you eat, it leaves you in peace."

"You're a little touched in the head, you know?"

"Yes. I do, and now you know, too." He heard her laugh as he closed the door.

Inside the bathroom, Rocky pressed the palms of his hands on the countertop, leaned forward, and stared at himself in the mirror over the vanity. He looked like hell warmed over. Bloodshot eyes and day old beard along with the smell of sweat and old whiskey made for a hideous picture of a homeless man. Heck, he bet a homeless dude looked and smelled much better.

His poor Horton shirt was a casualty of the day as well. He squeezed his eyes shut and prayed he could make it back to the bed and lay down before he passed out.

Rocky hadn't been so weak in a very long time. Not since those days after his injury when he was learning to walk again and would collapse each evening in exhaustion. His physical therapist always said he was pushing too hard, too fast but that was the way he'd always live his life. Too late to change that character trait.

And now he found himself doing the same thing in trying to solve Olivia's problems. He wished he could turn it off, but a guy couldn't change the hardwiring, could he? Tugging off his shirt, he took his second sink bath of the day. No way was he going to get in that double bed reeking of dirt and all the other debris of the trip back to the house. Sure, he wasn't going to be trying to turn her on, but he didn't want to chase her out of their hiding place either.

"Are you all right?" Olivia called through the door.

"Yeah. Almost done." Rocky glanced around the small room. No clean shirt miraculously appeared. He studied Horton. No. He couldn't put that back on. Now was the dilemma. He had on boxers, and that was it. And no shirt.

Would she think he was trying to seduce her by being almost naked? And more importantly, would his scars frighten her or lead to more questions he didn't want to answer?

There was nothing to do but leave the room. No matter what her reaction. He used the facilities and washed his hands.

When he stepped out and into the living area, her eyes widened, but all she said was, "I guess Horton didn't survive. Too bad. I think Bradford wanted to borrow it. You know, to wear to his next soirée."

"It *is* a statement piece," Rocky said, glad she was joking again.

Being sarcastic was part of her personality and, since she'd been in a state of anxiety, that had been repressed.

"I ate two of the granola bars, but there are more." Olivia looked at the floor.

Thinking she was embarrassed at his scarring, he

moved as quickly as his leg allowed and stopped at the bed. "I'm not hungry right now. I think the whiskey will be my dinner." He pointed to the mattress. "Which side do you prefer?"

"I can do either. You choose the one that will be the most comfortable for your leg." She still wasn't looking at him.

"This one will be fine." He sat and pulled the blanket over himself. Not that he was cold but that he wanted her to relax and quit acting like he'd bite her if she made eye contact.

This was completely out of character for her and it bothered him. She sure didn't need to be afraid of him. Lord knew she had enough men to fear. He sure didn't want to be one of them.

"I'll get the light then." Olivia strolled over to the light switch as if she were in no hurry to climb into bed with him.

He was used to women more eager to be with him than she was and he wasn't even going to touch her, so it was weird for her to be so reluctant. They were only going to sleep, for pity's sake.

When she finally made it back to the bed, she sat on the side in the dark.

Her voice a whisper, she asked, "Do you mind if I take off my slacks? I know I won't be comfortable sleeping in them."

"Sure. No problem. After all, I took mine off." He tried to keep his voice light hearted but found his throat tightening.

Now he had a picture in his head that might be impossible to get out.

Olivia with no pants? Yeah, that could be a problem.

Chapter 9

When she was tucked under the sheet, Olivia noticed that Graham had remained on top of it. Relieved that she wouldn't run into his bare leg and back as she slept, she relaxed slightly. This would be a first for her. Sleeping with a man without some kind of date and foreplay attached.

She bit back the snort that almost escaped. Now was not the time to be thinking of past conquests. Or should she say past mistakes?

The man beside her was head and shoulders above any other one she'd ever met in her life. For someone she didn't like less than forty-eight hours before, he sure had moved up in her estimation. He'd jumped right in to help her as if he had a stake in her survival himself.

And what kind of life *had* he led? The scar on his face was nothing compared to the horrific injury to his leg and foot, to say nothing of the gashes, both deep and shallow on his chest and back. She really wanted to ask but knew that would be stepping way over the bounds of propriety and man, her mother had ingrained those rules into her.

"I guess the moment of truth is here," he said.

"What's that?" Nervous about what he meant, she hoped her voice didn't quaver.

"Snore or no snore." He turned on his side, facing away from her and with his left leg on the top. Now she understood why he needed the side of the bed he chose.

She sat there for a few moments. Then leaned back on her pillow. Was she going to be able to do this? Could she actually fall asleep next to the man who suddenly seemed to be exuding way too much heat and testosterone for her comfort?

"Are you going to sit up all night?"

"No. Am I bothering you?"

"Kind of. How can I sleep if I'm worried you're going to not get any rest? I promise not to defile you while you're unconscious if that's your worry."

"Of course, it's not. I trust you."

"Then go to sleep. We don't know what tomorrow will bring, and we both need to be ready and able to act no matter what happens."

He was right. She needed to get over her sudden nervousness around him. After all, he was acting as if it were no big deal to be in a bed with her. She should do the same.

Settling in, she closed her eyes and drifted along, thinking of all that had transpired in the last day and a half. Graham's breathing became rhythmic.

Once she knew he was asleep, for some reason, that

relaxed her, and she gave herself up to the same thing.

She woke in what seemed only a few minutes but had to be much longer as the sky she could see through the one window was lighter than when she dozed off. But what was it that disturbed her sleep?

A sound?

Sitting straight up, Olivia panicked for a brief second.

Graham sat up as well. "What is it?"

"I heard something."

"This old house creaks. It's nothing. Go back to sleep."

"But what if it wasn't?"

"No one found this room before. They won't find it now."

"Who else knows about it? Anyone in town who could have told someone so the word could get out." For some strange reason, Olivia was almost in a panic. She couldn't figure it out. She'd been fine, and now she wasn't. A few tears slid down her cheeks. "I know I'm being irrational, but I can't stop my brain from imagining all kinds of craziness."

He wiped her tears with the pads of his thumbs. "It's all right. You've had a hard day. It's understandable that you'd be spooked."

His gentleness was her undoing. She'd been holding herself together for so long all by herself, and the dam broke as soon as he touched her face.

Graham put his arms around her. Olivia sobbed against his bare chest as he patted her back.

Eventually, she realized what she was doing and pulled away from him. "Sorry." She ran her hand across her eyes and sniffled deeply. "Didn't mean to bring my pity party to the room."

"Why do I get the feeling you haven't done that in a very long time?"

"Done what?"

"Let yourself go. Just cry out all the emotion and fear you've been feeling."

"You're right. I've been holding myself together for too many years. It gets rough when you've got no one to confide in. Believe me, it's not a life I'd wish on any-one."

"But you're going back to that as soon as I can get you out of town, right?"

"I have no choice, do I? At least for the next two years. Once I change that beneficiary, I'll be safe. I plan to return here since it's the place I've felt the most at home since my father died and I left our houses in New York."

"What if we could figure a way for you to stay now? Would you?"

"I'd like to. Very much. But I'd be scared the whole time that something would happen to me, and I'd proba-bly end up in a mental ward."

"Let's think about it for a day or two. Maybe we can put some pressure on in New York for an investigation into your mother's condition and how she got that way."

"I tried that before I disappeared."

"When I read the article in the paper, I noticed that,

but I also saw you were only twenty-two or twenty-three when you left. Maybe they'd take you more seriously since you're older. Especially since your mother has been incapacitated so much longer." Graham ran his hand down her arm. "Sleep now. We'll talk more in the morning."

"Okay. I'm not optimistic, but you're right. Running is no fun, and if I could find another way, I would certainly stay and fight."

"First, we rest, second, we find a way out of here. Once we get down the road a piece, we'll decide whether to head to New York and face the enemy." He kissed her forehead. "I promise, we're safe up here, and any sounds you hear are just the building settling."

"I hope you're right."

"If I'm not, my friend, Mr. Glock, is right here." Graham patted the mattress.

"When did you put it there? I didn't see you with a gun."

"I had it when I came up from leaving the truck. I got it from where I keep it in the kitchen. Suffice it to say, it's handy."

"I'm not a big fan of firearms, but since I've been in Texas and learned everyone is carrying, I've become more tolerant."

"I noticed the look on your face in the bar when you had the wrench. I'd say you really don't like guns. But I agree about being more tolerant since moving here. Not being a native myself, it took me a while to realize everyone had one in the glove compartment in their trucks."

"Where *are* you from originally?"

"Tomorrow, Olivia. Ask me tomorrow." He smiled and settled back down on the bed. With his arm over his eyes, he said, "Good night."

She sat there a moment then stood and made her way to the bathroom to wash the tears off her face.

Inside, she thought about the conversations they'd had. It dawned on her that every time she asked him something about himself, he either changed the subject or put her off. Determined to find out more information on his past, she scrubbed her face clean and then returned to the bed and was soon drifting off again.

In what seemed like minutes, the sun peeked through the window. Olivia rolled over and ran her hand over Graham's side of the bed. It was empty.

She almost jumped out of bed in fear, her eyes scanning the room. He was gone.

She dashed over to the bathroom and knocked on the door. The light wasn't showing under the bottom, but maybe he was inside.

No one answered.

Almost in a frenzy, Olivia headed to the door leading down the secret staircase. She flung it open, grabbed the discarded chair leg as her weapon, and headed down the steps, determined to find Graham.

At the bend around the chimney, she met him coming back up. He had a tray in his hands and had somewhere found a pair of jeans and a shirt. She suddenly became conscious of the fact that she only had on her shirt, bra, and panties.

In her haste to find him, she hadn't pulled on her slacks.

"Can you turn around and let me follow you?" he asked. "This is precarious, but I figured we needed something hot to eat."

"You scared me to death. I didn't know where you were or if someone got to you and was coming for me next."

"I like your weapon of choice, but all is well."

"My real weapon of choice is my Stillson wrench."

"Yeah. I heard all about that. I'm sorry I was outside and missed the whole show. I bet you were magnificent as you swung that thing down on that punk's shoulder."

"I wish I hadn't done it and I also wish people weren't so eager to video everything and post it online. I'd still be secretly hidden and safe."

"But at what cost? You don't know what those guys would've done. They could've robbed everyone in the place or even hurt some of the patrons. Hostage situations sometimes happen in robberies as well. Don't ever doubt you did the right thing.

He nodded at the stairs. "Go. Let's eat before I drop this and scald myself."

Once they were back in the room, he set the tray on the side table. He picked up a tea pot and poured what looked like a mixture of milk and hot water into first one cup and then a second one. Handing her a spoon and one of the containers, he said, "Instant oatmeal. I hope you like that kind of thing. I didn't want to spend too much time in the kitchen. No need to take unnecessary risks."

Olivia stirred her breakfast. Even if she wasn't fond of oatmeal, the heat of it and the fact that it filled her belly, would have made a fan of her for at least the day.

She took a seat on the bed and covered her bare legs with the sheet as she ate. The oatmeal was tasty and for a few moments, they each busied themselves with the meal, not talking.

"I realized while I was downstairs that I somehow left my cell phone in the truck," Graham said.

"Not that you had anything else on your mind or weren't in any pain."

"Yeah, but I should've gotten it. We sure could use it. I'm sure whoever is after you has checked to see what cars I have registered to me. I could bet they've got my house staked out and my vehicles either marked with tracking devices or some way to follow us. If I had a cell phone, I could call and reserve a rental."

"No." Olivia shook her head. "The phone would be traceable, too and even if you could reserve a car, how would we get to it?"

"You're right. I didn't think about that. Duh." He smacked his forehead. "Wait. I know. I have an idea."

Eager to hear what he had to say, she leaned forward. "What?"

"I have a hay baler parked near here. If we can get to it, we can at least get off the property. And via a way that's not near the main road that most people travel."

"Then let's try that."

"I'll wash these dishes, and you put the bed back in the wall with the table in front of it. Once we get those tasks done, we can go." He placed his cup on the tray, picked it up and walked to her where she could place her empty cup on top.

Moving toward the bathroom, Olivia could tell he felt much better since he was walking with no discernable limp.

Over his shoulder, he said, "While I'm in here, you might want to put on your pants since I doubt you'd be comfortable in the baler in those panties."

Mortified, she sat still for a few moments. Good grief, she hadn't even thought about how thin and tiny they were. What had she left to the imagination? Her cheeks burned. Not sure if she was mad or embarrassed, she took advantage of him being out of the room to make herself presentable.

Tugging on her slacks quickly, she put the Murphy bed back how it went and was ready to leave as soon as Graham returned.

∾∾

It was all Rocky could do to hold himself together when Olivia came down the stairs in her panties. Since it had been dark when she took off her trousers the night before, even though he knew, in concept, she was next to him in the bed with just her undies on, it didn't register exactly how hot she was.

Her legs seemed to go on forever, and the silk was sheer and enticing. He'd had to avert his eyes and was physically relieved when she sat with the sheet over her.

Taking his time while washing the cups, he used the moment to get himself under control. This was not the time to get distracted by the woman. All he needed to do was help her survive. He did *not* need to get bogged down in lust for her. That was not kosher, and it was always the path to hell for him.

Determined to block the memory of her loveliness, he dried the dishes, replaced them on the tray and returned to the main room.

"Here's the plan," he said. "We'll go downstairs. You stay behind me at all times. I'll have the Glock and be ready to use it if I need to."

"And how far is the baler?"

"Down the way close to three-hundred yards."

"That far?"

"Yeah. Sorry." He smiled to try to ease the tension. "If I'd known what was going to happen, I'd have parked it closer."

"Very funny. Now you sound like the Rocky I know."

"Are we back to Rocky then?"

"Huh? What do you mean?" Olivia shook her head.

"You've been calling me Graham."

"Does it bother you?"

"No. I actually quite like it." He ducked his head so she couldn't see how much he wanted her to keep calling him by his given name.

"How long have you been called Rocky?"

"Since I joined the army. The men in service always come up with nicknames. It's almost as bad as the acronyms they're famous for. When I was in boot camp, I was called Rockford, and that, eventually, got shortened to Rock and then Rocky."

"Rock sounds stronger. More manly. It also fits you better than Rocky."

Pleased that she thought he was manly, even after his cry baby moments the night before when he thought his leg would fall off from the agony, he smiled. "There's a story behind the change from Rock to Rocky."

"Please tell me. You have a bad habit of changing the subject every time we get close to something personal about you."

"I already have bad habits?"

"Already? You forget I've known you for a long time."

He arched his eyebrows. "But never at this level. I mean, we've slept together now."

"You will not bandy that about town. Whether I'm here or not."

"Come on. We need to get moving." Graham glanced around the room. It was tidy enough. Time to go.

Olivia sat on the chair closest to her. "Nope. Not until you tell me the story. About the name change."

He let out a deep sigh. "All right. It's not that big a deal."

"It's only a big deal because you're actually sharing information."

"If I tell you, then we can go?"

"Yes." She crossed her arms. "Are you delaying?"

"No. I'm kind of in a hurry."

"To get rid of me?"

"Of course not. To avoid your pursuers."

She laughed. "Then start talking, buddy."

Graham leaned on the wall. "Some new guy came into our unit. A real hot dog. He started calling me Hudson."

She tilted her head, obviously confused. "Hudson?"

"Yes. As in Rock Hudson. And he would flounce around. It made me mad. Not that I wouldn't want to be equated with the actor but that this bozo would make fun of gays. I've always had friends of both sexual persuasions, and he offended me with his comments. Finally, one day, I lashed out and told him off. The other guys decided to change my name to Rocky and sing the theme song from that movie when I walked by. I didn't like that either, but at least it wasn't rude."

"What ended up happening to the guy? Did he get out of the service, too?"

"Not in a good way. He got blown up by an IED."

"Oh, my God, that's awful."

"Sure is, and I wouldn't wish it on anyone, jerk or not." Now they were getting into dangerous territory. He needed to change the subject before he let himself think back on that day too much more. That was a closed compartment. "Can we move on now?"

"Just one more question,"

"What?" Graham hoped whatever she wanted to know didn't involve particulars of the event that changed his life forever.

"When you got out, why didn't you drop the nickname and introduce yourself as Graham when you met new people?"

"I don't know. Maybe because by then, I'd become Rocky and Graham seemed to be a long way away. Another lifetime—different man—if you will." Now he'd given away more than he ever intended. He needed to shut his trap.

Olivia stood and approached him. When she was in reaching distance, she placed her palm on his right cheek. "You poor dear man. You've been through a lot, haven't you? No wonder you're prickly most of the time."

Doing his best not to let her see how her words touched him, he covered her hand with his. "Enough talking. We need to move on. It's still early, and, hopefully, we can get out of here in one piece.

"I'm confident we will. You're obviously well-trained, and I trust you."

That put additional pressure on. Somehow, when she was more standoffish, he didn't care if he had her approval or not but now that she said she trusted him to get her to safety, it became more vital than it had before. He sure didn't want to disappoint her. Like he had Clara.

"Remind me of that later." Graham gave her a grim smile. "On the other side of this mission." He opened the door. "Let's go. Stick close. Like the paste you used in first grade to hold your artwork to construction paper."

"Nice analogy." Olivia hooked her index finger into his back belt loop.

"Came to me because I was making hand-turkeys with the kids at the hospital."

"Hand-turkeys?" she asked as they went down the stairs.

"You know. When you trace your hand?"

"Can't say I've ever done that."

"I'll show you when we're safe, but for now, you'll have to let go of my jeans so I can squeeze past this chimney. Once we're in the dining room, take hold again. I think that's a good plan. Harder to separate us this way."

He pulled out the Glock before opening the secret door. "Stay behind me as I clear the way. When I was here earlier, there was no one around. I'm pretty sure that's still true but just in case, be alert."

They made their way through the house with no issues. Graham decided to go out the rear exit as it was closer to the hay baler.

In a few moments, they were on the way across the field toward the big red machine. The scariest part of the journey was those three football-field lengths of open space.

If anyone had eyes on them, they'd be at their most vulnerable.

Surprisingly, they made it with ease.

Once they were settled inside the cab, Olivia asked, "Now where?"

"We try to get to my truck and get my phone. Then we call and reserve a car at the airport."

"How do we get to the airport to get it without being seen?"

"We don't. We call Sam to get it for us and park it

near the county line. Then we drive this over there, jump in it and go."

"Won't that put him in danger?"

"No, because the more I think about it, the more I realize we need him to reserve it in his own name. There'd be no reason to put it in mine."

"Don't they have rules about who can drive a rental car? Like only the person on the lease?"

"If you're going to worry about breaking terms in a contract now after hiding and going under a fake name all this time, I worry about you."

"What's that supposed to mean?" Now, this looked like the old Olivia. Mad at something he said and like a dog pulling on a lead that was on too tight.

"Don't go getting all offended. I merely meant to point out that the wrong person driving a rental car for the short distance we plan to drive it is nothing compared to dying before your thirtieth birthday."

"Oh. When you put it like that, then, okay."

"Let's get to the truck." He cranked the hay baler and with her seated almost on his lap since the cab wasn't that large, he moved forward, lurching across the terrain.

The gun sat on the metal piece where the steering wheel was installed. He wanted it near and handy in case they needed it.

Shocked when they made it to the truck with ease, Graham turned to Olivia before he opened the door to the cab. "Stay right here. Don't get out. I'm going to leave the gun here with you. Do you know how to use it?"

"No. I don't. Take it with you. You might need it before I would."

"They aren't after me."

"Good point but I have no idea what to do with it,
and I'd probably do myself harm rather than them, so you
take it."

"I'm not comfortable with that, but I see you're not
giving me a choice." He took it from its resting place and
stepped out of the cab. "Be right back."

In the truck, he found his phone right where he left it.
In the cup holder. Taking it in his hand, he grabbed the
charger from the USB slot as well.

Relieved there was no one around, Graham turned
toward the hay baler. Olivia sat in the cab, but she wasn't
waiting calmly.

She waved her arms frantically and pointed behind
him.

Chapter 10

Olivia couldn't believe it. A car came toward them. She knew when she told Graham to take the gun with him that something bad was going to happen. What was she going to do? He was taking too long inside the truck, and this stupid hay baler cab was obviously soundproof since he didn't seem to hear her warning.

If she got out, she'd be vulnerable. If she stayed, he would be. Torn about what to do, she let out a deep breath, yelled again, and waved her arms to get his attention. Surely he would see her, get up here with her, and drive this thing.

Then it dawned on her. *She* could drive it and run over that car coming toward them.

Olivia moved over to grab the steering wheel at the same time Graham placed his foot on the step to come up to the cab.

She tried to move the vehicle forward but only succeeded in knocking it out of gear. It lurched and stopped.

She noticed Graham at the window beside her. He almost stumbled and grabbed onto the door to keep from falling.

Dear God, she knew she was going to make it worse. Why in the world hadn't she gotten out, gotten the phone, and left him to drive the blasted thing?

The door opened. Graham slid inside. "Move over. What were you thinking?"

Getting out of his way, she made herself as small as she could in the corner of the cab.

"I thought I could run over that vehicle and buy us some time."

He handed her the phone. "Call Sam and tell him we need a rental. Now."

"How will we get away from those guys?"

"Just like you said. We'll run them down."

Something hit the side of the hay baler. It made a ping sound.

"What was that?" she asked.

"Bullet."

"Oh, God. What should we do?"

"Dial the phone. Call Sam."

"What about the police?"

"That, too." Graham pressed the gas pedal.

It looked to Olivia as if he laid it down as far as it would go. Just her luck to be in a lumbering old heap of metal when the bullets were flying.

Why couldn't she be in a turbo-charged Mach drive Indy car or something equally as fast? One that could out-run ammo.

Olivia made the call first to the police. Sure, Graham

told her the opposite order, but it made more sense to her to call law enforcement first.

More bullets zinged past, but the men clearly weren't marksmen as none of the shots got even close to Olivia and Graham.

The car headed straight at them. Graham didn't flinch. A weird grin on his face, he said, "Ever played chicken?"

"No. Can't say I have."

"Now you can say you did and more importantly, that you won." He kept going and plowed right into the smaller vehicle.

He threw the baler into reverse and then rammed the car again.

When he did it for the third time, over the sound of more gunfire, steam came from the car's engine and out the sides of the hood.

"Those fools are going to set themselves on fire with all that shooting." Graham rammed the car for the fourth time.

Fire did break out then, and two men rolled out of the car, one on each side.

Olivia dialed Sam's number as Graham backed up once more, turned the baler away from the car, and back toward the house.

"Where are we going? We're not going to wait for the police?"

Sam's phone rang. When he answered, Olivia told him about the need for a car and where to leave it.

Sam promised to get the rental as soon as he could.

"No, we're not waiting for the deputies. They'll want us to come to the station and give a statement. That will take way too long. Those two clowns will come up with some story why they were out here, and all that'll happen is we'd be delayed. That would give a chance to the person behind all this to find someone else to get to you." Graham patted her leg. "This is the time to move. Get some distance between us and them."

"How do we know they don't have someone else already lined up to come after us?" She paused before changing her mind. "Come after me, I mean."

"We don't. That's why we need to move and do it now."

"I'm trusting you."

"I know. You said that, and I'm taking you seriously. I want us both to survive this."

"And I appreciate it because there's a lot of living I want to do."

"Call Sam back and have him get Sharon to go by your place and get the bag you packed. Can't hurt to have your clothes with you."

"What about yours?"

"I'm easy. I can pick up some things on the road."

"I could do the same you know. I've left all my things before."

"I imagine you have a stash of funds somewhere at your house that you might need."

She remembered the bearer bonds then. How had they slipped her mind? Gee. She'd have thought they would be foremost in her brain. True, she had the money from the safe deposit box in her tote bag, but those bonds might be needed. "You're right. I'll call him and ask him to swing by for it."

"No. Get Sharon to get it and take it to the bar. He can get it there. That way if anyone decides one of them may help you, they wouldn't know which one. If they see her at your house, that may buy us some more time. If there are more of them in town, that is. We have no way to know how many are here or how many they have lined up to show when things get hotter."

Olivia was surprised at the idea. "You think things are going to get hotter?"

"I have no doubt. That back there was pretty intense. How would they have explained why they shot you if they'd been successful? This is way past the subtly murderous poisoning or whatever was done to your mother to put her into a coma. And it's not something that could be explained like the car issues you had before you left New York. A hit and run or failed brakes are way different than a body riddled with .45 slugs."

"Do you *have* to be so graphic?"

"Yeah, I do. We need to remember what's at stake. Too often, people forget." Graham kept driving, not letting up for one second.

Olivia made the call to Sharon, and once she'd convinced her she was okay, Sharon agreed to get the suitcase and give it to Sam.

It took the hay baler a long time to get to the rendezvous point, but they still got there before Sam. When they arrived, Graham stepped to the ground then assisted her.

Once her feet were on the ground, she almost kissed it. That baler was a rough ride. Olivia bet her rear had met each and every rut in that field. And there were quite a number of them.

If she didn't think Graham would look at her as if she were completely crazy, she would have rubbed her bottom until it felt better.

"You doing all right?" he asked. The fact that he held the gun in his right hand, hanging down by his thigh, didn't do much to make her feel at ease but since she was alive, she was okay.

"I'm fine. I think so anyway."

"We're ahead of the game. It's going to be good."

A car came down the road. A small dark blue Honda SUV.

Olivia glanced at Graham in a panic. "How do we know who this is? Sam didn't tell me what kind of vehicle he was getting."

"I think it's safe. Look." Graham pointed.

Sam hung out the passenger side, waving his right arm.

She shook her head. "Good grief, he might as well announce he's coming."

"I guess he thought it would be better than having his head shot off."

"Does he think you're trigger happy?" She smiled as the SUV came to a stop on the shoulder of the road.

"No, but he *does* know me pretty well. I think he'd want to make himself known sooner rather than later."

"Who's driving?"

"I can't tell, but I'm sure it's someone we can trust or Sam wouldn't have that big grin."

The doors opened. Sam got out on the passenger side followed by Russell on the driver's side.

Olivia let out a pleased sigh. Good. Things were looking up for at least one of her friends' lives. Sam had long had a crush on Russell so seeing the two of them together made her happy.

She took three long strides to Sam's side. Hugging him, she said, "Thanks for being such a great friend. You've saved us for sure."

"No problem." Sam held her for a second then took a long look at her. "Girl, I have to say, thank God you asked me to bring some other clothes. You need them."

"Thanks and I love you, too."

"You know I adore you no matter what but as soon as you find a place to land, you need a long shower and some make-up refreshing time."

"I'll keep that in mind." Olivia laughed the first real laugh she'd had since the night those punks walked into her bar. Sam was always good for morale.

"We need to go. Thanks, Sam." Graham shook Sam's hand and then did the same for Russell. "Sorry I can't offer you the best ride, but if you take that hay baler back to my barn, you can drive the 'vette." He handed a set of keys to Russell. "They're all there. Use whatever you want. The car or the bikes."

"Oh, speaking of keys, here's the one to the bar. You and Sharon run it for me until I can get back." Tears filled Olivia's eyes, blinding her for a moment. "No matter how long it takes. You're both already on the bank accounts so be sure to keep the doors open."

"Can you take care of my livestock as well while we're gone?" Graham asked Sam.

"Of course. I've done it before and am always glad to help."

Graham shook Sam's hand. "Thanks."

"Come back soon. We'll miss you." Sam hugged Olivia and whispered in her ear, "And you need to come back so we can gossip about Russell."

"You bet. I'm so happy for you."

"Thanks for encouraging me." Sam let her go and clapped Graham on the shoulder. "Take good care of our girl."

"I plan on it. Be careful, and we'll be in touch about where we leave the rental."

"Thanks." Sam took hold of Russell's hand. "Come home as soon as you can."

"We will." Graham took Olivia by the elbow. "Thanks to you both." He led her to the SUV, and they got in.

After they buckled up, Graham drove them away.

She looked behind her as they moved down the pavement. "Do you think they'll be okay?"

"Absolutely. They have no information about where we're going. There would be no purpose in harming them, and it seems to me the people who are after you aren't in the game to hurt people for the sake of hurting people. They're in it for the money."

"I think I agree with that. I hope that's the case. I

love that guy, and I'd hate for him to be harmed because of me," Olivia said.

"I'm with you on that."

"Except it wouldn't be him getting hurt because of you."

"Now it would because he's driving my hay baler."

Olivia laughed. "No. I'm quite sure it's Russell driving your rig. No way would Sam be able to handle that piece of machinery. Trust me, I know this."

"I think you're right." Graham turned down the next highway. "Where to? We need to pick a place to change cars and then where we're going until we can prepare to confront your mother's husband in New York."

"So far, you've kept me alive, so I'm going to leave it in your hands."

"All right then. Let's head northeast and see where we get before lunch. We'll leave the car somewhere like a mall and let Sam know where it is a few hours later. That way, if someone decides to follow him, we'll be long gone when he gets to it."

"Makes sense." She yawned. "I didn't sleep very well last night. If I doze off, don't get insulted."

"No worries. I noticed you were restless, but I wasn't sure if it was because you were in bed with such a handsome guy that you couldn't settle down."

"That was totally it. You caught me." She giggled but realized that he was actually right in a way. There was that moment when she was so vitally aware of his masculinity that it made her knees shake.

"Good to know. I'll make sure we get separate rooms

tonight so you can forget how amazing I am in bed."

"No. Let's stay in the same room." She looked over at him. "Not that I'm propositioning you, but I don't think I can be alone. I'd be terrified. We can get two beds."

Graham reached over and touched her lightly on the thigh, then took his hand away. "I was teasing. Of course, we're going to stay together. Now, shut your eyes. I'll wake you for lunch."

His kindness affected her again, and it was all she could do not to cry. He had the softest voice when he was trying to ease her fears, and it made her vulnerable. She wasn't used to that. She was an independent, fierce woman usually. This sensation of being grateful to such an emotional degree when someone showed her the least little bit of kindness was new, and she wasn't sure she liked it. At all.

ↄ◌ↄ

As she slept and he drove farther north, Graham cast a sidelong glance at her every few miles. He'd somehow let her in past all the guards he'd set up in his heart. In the years since Clara's death, he'd only allowed himself the freedom to care about and dote affection on the children he met in his volunteer work at the hospitals.

Children and his farm animals. They were easy. No expectations other than a treat once in a while and a hug and pat on the back. Grown-ups were much more complicated.

Sure, a man could have his drinking and card-playing buddies, and while he might care for them, the tie was loose and not dependent. This caring for another woman was something he'd told himself was never going to happen and now, somehow, he'd let her in.

He wanted to beat the steering wheel in frustration and anger at himself, but he couldn't bring himself to disturb her.

That elicited a snort.

Olivia started and sat up. She ran a hand over her eyes. "How long did I sleep?"

"A couple of hours. We're coming into a town. Do you want to eat something?"

"Absolutely. You're a pretty awesome instant oatmeal stirrer, and the dinner of granola bars was exceptional, but I could sure use a real meal."

"Same here." He grinned in her direction. "But thanks for the compliments on my culinary skills."

"Somehow—and don't ask me how it happened— even my least favorite food, nasty old oatmeal, tasted pretty good with you."

"I'll take that as a compliment, even though you called my food nasty."

"Oh, I didn't mean your oatmeal in particular. I just never eat it anymore since I don't have to. I had a nanny as a kid that thought it was not only essential to eat for breakfast every day no matter the season but also thought it was a cure-all for whatever ails you. So, in addition to having had way too much of it on a daily basis, I also exceeded my quota when I was sick."

"Funny. I feel the same way about Seven-Up. If I drink it, I start to feel sick because that was what my mother always gave us to settle our stomachs."

"Isn't weird how we get these food and drink aversions?"

"Sure is but speaking of food, where do you want to eat?" Graham glanced out the car window. "I see an IHOP, a couple of burger joints and a Pizza Hut. Or did you want to go more upscale?"

"Absolutely not. I haven't had a bath in over twenty-four hours, and as Sam said, I need some make-up refreshment, so fast food is best, I'm afraid."

"Let's do the IHOP then. They have both breakfast and lunch." He grinned. "You never know, they may have oatmeal."

"And Seven-Up." She playfully punched his arm. "If you make me order oatmeal, I'm ordering you all the Seven-Up in the place."

"Deal. No making each other eat or drink evil concoctions." Graham pulled into the parking lot of the IHOP. "Unless I get sick. Then I'll be wanting the Seven-Up."

"I'll keep that in mind." She opened her door as soon as he parked the Honda.

Inside the restaurant, Graham asked for a booth in the back.

He sat so he could watch the door. Not that he thought anyone was still on their trail. He'd made sure of that as they drove along. No noticeable tails and no similar cars that had stayed in their general vicinity.

He was pretty sure they were in the clear, but it didn't hurt to be safe.

After they ordered and the waitress was gone, Olivia leaned forward. "What's next? Did you figure out where to leave the car?"

"This is a nice sized town. I'll ask the waitress for directions to the mall. While we're there, I'll get another phone. One of those that has no contract. I've had mine off with the battery out so it can't be traced. We can leave it in the car for Sam to take back. That way, we won't be tempted to use it."

"I'm so glad I never got dependent on one. It's easier to stay off people's radar that way."

"We're going to need something with Internet access if we're going to be prepared for what's ahead."

"What do you mean?"

The waitress took that moment to return with their coffees. "Your orders will be up in a few minutes."

"Before you go, can I ask how to get to the mall?"

"Oh, that's easy." The waitress smiled at Graham and leaned her hip on the table. "It's right down the road you turned off of to get into our parking lot. Just go back out to the left when you leave, and, in about a mile and a half, it'll be on your right."

"Thanks. You've been very helpful."

"My name's Alicia, and if you and your friend here will be in town for a couple of days, I'd love to take you out and show you some of the sights."

"Thanks. I'll think about it. I'm not sure where we're staying yet, but I know where to find you." Graham decided it was better to pretend he might be interested in the woman than for her to be alone with his food and mad at him for brushing her off. No telling what she might do to it if she didn't like his answer to her come on.

As soon as they were alone, Olivia said, "You made yourself a conquest there. Although she doesn't seem to be your type."

"Can't hurt to be nice." He laughed. "And what do you know about my type anyway?"

"You forget. I own a bar, and I've seen you with a number of women over the past two years."

"But never more than once or maybe twice with the same one, right?"

"Right." She studied him for a moment. "You know what I used to think about you?"

"What's that?"

"That you were a player. Couldn't settle for one girl because you were too busy being with any girl who struck your fancy and then dumping them."

"You really thought I was that kind of guy?"

"Sure. Who wouldn't? You played it to the hilt. In and out of the bar almost every time with a different lady and, when you were alone, you flirted with every girl. Always regaling them with stories about how you got that scar on your face—none of which I ever believed, by the way."

"What? You didn't believe I was a swashbuckling pirate?"

"You're as much a pirate as Johnny Depp."

"Well, that's something I guess." He stroked his

chin. "Wait a second. You said what you *used* to think of me. Has your opinion changed?"

She nodded. "It has."

"And now what do you think?" He wasn't sure he wanted to hear it. He'd presumed it would be a change for the better. Never having really been a ladies man but merely a loner, it amused him to hear she'd thought him a player. Truth be known, he didn't sleep around. His wounds and scars tended to turn women away.

The waitress returned. She almost reverently placed his ham and egg sandwich with hash browns in front of him then practically slammed Olivia's plate of roast beef and mashed potatoes in her general direction.

As soon as she was gone, Olivia laughed. "I've never seen gravy slosh quite like that on a plate. I think the lady doesn't like me." She picked up her fork. "Either that or she thinks I'm the competition."

"The woman needs to watch how she treats diners. She could be losing tips if she keeps paying better attention to the men at the table than the women. She should know the woman decides on the amount of the tip."

"Who made up that rule?"

He shrugged before picking up his sandwich. "It's just the way it always was when I was dating."

"You say that like you don't date any longer."

"Which leads us back to that player versus non-player conversation." Graham took a bite of his sandwich. Part of the runny egg plopped out on his plate.

"In the time I've spent with you, I've come to realize you really aren't one. Rather, I think you hide the sensitive soul you are behind bravado and surrounding yourself with women. Ones you have no intention of getting involved with. I haven't worked out the reason for that, but I think it'll come to me the more we're together."

She was already a lot closer to the truth than he was comfortable with. How was she so savvy in the psychology of an old war horse?

"Sounds like you've given me a lot of thought."

"I had a lot of time on my own while you hid the truck and worked your way back to the house. What else was there for me to do except think?" Olivia scooped up a forkful of roast.

He watched her chew while he had another bite of his sandwich that was threatening to fall completely apart in his hands.

Her words hit a bit close to home. He *did* tend to see a lot of women in order to not be obligated to one in particular. It was an easier way to be sure no one would start to feel they had a special place in his life, much less in his heart. Staying aloof and apart was vital to keeping himself sane.

Taking no risks in getting to know any one woman deeply meant he couldn't hurt one or drive them to hurt themselves. And now here he was, falling for one.

"You've gotten awfully quiet," Olivia said.

"Just eating and thinking about where we're heading from here."

She smiled and sipped her coffee. "That all?"

"You bet." He raised his hand to signal the waitress. "Let's get the bill and head over to the mall. I'd like to get that phone and some changes of clothes."

"Good idea. I'm glad Sam brought my suitcase, so once we find a place to stay, I can freshen up."

"We need to get quite a few more miles behind us before we can do that."

The waitress came over. "We need our ticket," Graham said.

"Sure." She dug around in her apron pocket and pulled out her order pad. Pulling off their sheet, she also handed him another piece of paper. "This one has my phone number in case you want to take me up on my offer to show you around while you're here."

To be polite, he took them both. He made a big production of placing the one with her contact information in his pocket.

He was rewarded with a big smile.

Casting a glance at Olivia to gauge her reaction, he was pleased to see she was taking the interaction in stride. She didn't seem the least bit jealous or unhappy about it. Of course, she also knew they weren't staying in town so she didn't have anything to worry about with this lady.

One thing he couldn't stand was jealousy. It was a vicious emotion, and too many people died from it. He hated the things it made normally rational and sober people do to each other.

Finding out this lady he'd learned to care for was at least able to laugh about another woman flirting boldly with him in front of her went a long way in raising Olivia in his estimation. Of course, it wasn't like they were involved with each other or anything like that.

"Time to get going," Olivia said. She looked at the waitress. "Thanks for being so nice to my brother. He just made parole from the Texas State Penitentiary, and hooking up with you would be the first woman he's had in—" She turned to Graham. "—what is it? Like ten years or something?"

"More like eight. Believe me, I've counted the days, and I didn't expect to find someone so willing so fast." He patted his back pocket. "Once we're done at the mall getting me some civilian clothes, I'll be using this number."

The waitress backed away. "Sorry. I just remembered a previous date. Good luck."

It was all Graham could do not to laugh. Olivia was a minx. That was sure.

As soon as the bill was paid, with the waitress keeping her distance but clearly gossiping about him behind her hand to her coworker, they stepped out into the parking lot.

He unlocked the SUV. "You're something else, lady."

"Did you see her face? I wasn't sure if she was more afraid of the fact that you were in prison or that you hadn't had sex in eight years."

"Who said I hadn't had sex? I'll have you know there was a super-hot guy on my cellblock. Who could've resisted him?'

Olivia shook her head as she opened her car door. "Only you could come up with a whole scenario about what was going on in this fake prison I just invented."

He winked at her as she made eye contact with him over the top of the car. "Maybe it's all true."

"Yeah. Right. Let's get out of here and find that mall. The sooner we find you some new clothes and us a different car, the sooner I can get that long-awaited shower."

"I'm waiting for you to get in."

Instead of responding, she did as instructed and slid into her seat. By the time he got in himself, she was buckled in and ready to go.

"Let's go by the library first. I want to use their Internet and do a little research." Graham started the vehicle and revved the accelerator a little.

"What are we going to look up?"

"A few things. Among them, my sister's new address."

"You don't know your sister's address? I got the impression you two were close since you had so many memories of your grandmother's house and you said she had the china."

"Being close doesn't always mean *staying* close. Things can happen that screw that up."

"Will you tell me about them?"

"No. Not now. Maybe later." Graham prayed his expression would put her off from asking. He sure hoped so. He wasn't ready to share that information.

Chapter 11

The forbidding look that came over Graham's previously open and laughing countenance told Olivia she needed to back off. She shut her mouth and watched as he drove down the highway. The waitress had told them the mall was right down the street but now he wanted to go to the library. How he was going to find that, she had no idea.

He pulled into a gas station. "I'm going to fill the tank for Sam, and while I'm at it, I'll go inside and find out where the library is."

"Let me pump while you go ask. I'd go, but since I'm not good with directions, I figure it'll be better for you to talk to the guy since you'll be the one driving."

"I can do both. Sit tight." He stepped out and before she could even open her door to help, he had the nozzle out and in the tank.

She suppressed a smile. Yep. He was as macho as they came. No way would he stand by while a lady pumped fuel for him.

When he returned, he tossed a couple of bottles of water on the seat. "We might need these later."

"Did you get the location of the library?"

"I did. It's not too far." Graham put the car in gear and then pulled into traffic.

It took fifteen minutes to find the library and park. "Come on. Let's make this quick. I'd like to get another car and leave this one at the mall."

"And get that untraceable phone, right?"

"Right."

Inside the library, they had to wait a few minutes for an available computer, but once Graham was able to log on, he made short work of his Google search.

When Olivia saw the name he typed in, she shook her head in confusion. "I thought we were going to find your sister's address?"

"I am. We are." He clicked on the third icon down when the results page came up.

"Your sister works for Senator Matthews? Of New York?" Stunned, as she had no idea he had a New York connection, she sat down hard on the chair that was luckily beside where she stood, or she would've ended up on the floor.

Graham gave her the grin she'd begun to wish to see more often. The one that made him look younger and made his scar less noticeable since the smile was so megawatt. "You might say that."

"What does *that* mean?" Olivia stared at the screen as a large family portrait of the senator, her spouse, three children and even a dog filled the screen.

Then she saw it. Even though she'd met the senator at various functions back when the woman was a newly elected member of the state house of representatives, in a vacuum, Olivia would never had imagined the dignified, quiet lady to be any relation to the large pony-tailed man she'd been hanging out with for the last few days.

Now that she had them side-by-side so to speak, she caught the resemblance immediately. The lady was practically his twin. Great for him since he was handsome, not so great for her since she was a woman. She was still striking-looking but not feminine in feature at all.

"I see," Olivia said.

"Kind of obvious, yeah? My dad had some pretty dominant genes." Graham was grinning again. "Poor girl. She never had a chance."

"Looks like she did all right for herself."

"When no one wants to date you as a teen girl, you change your focus from boys and pretty dresses to saving the world. I'm really quite proud of her. She's got guts."

"And found a husband, after all." Olivia studied the man. He was a thin, wiry person of average height and looks but the three children had turned out nicely.

"She did, and he's a good egg. I like him."

"But you don't get along with her?"

The closed look came back over his face. "Let's just say there's a lot of history there."

He scrolled down the page, looking for an address, Olivia presumed. He'd sure seemed to care about his sister when he was staring at the photo. That made Olivia even more curious about the reasons for their split but she had to trust he'd tell her when he was ready. Or maybe she'd learn it from the senator herself when they showed up on her doorstep.

"See an address?"

"Nope but I do recognize the house."

"Oh, good. Is it where she lived when you last saw her?"

"No. It seems she bought the old family homestead when Dad died."

"How did you not know? Wouldn't it have gone through his probate estate?"

"Someone else bought it then. She must've gotten them to sell it to her." He sent a quick email to Sam telling him where to find the car.

"Good idea to do that here rather than using your phone. I hate that phones can be tracked like that. One of the reasons I refuse to have one."

"You may need one someday, and I hope that you can get one soon. When you don't need to fear being found." Graham erased the history of the computer and turned to her. "And now, we have a long drive."

"What about just taking a plane? Save some time?"

"I know you have a fake passport, but I don't. I'm not sure what kind of access your pursuers have to flight manifests, so I'm reluctant to go that route."

"There's a solution to that."

"What? I'm not going to try to find a forger here in town to get an ID." He smiled. She hoped it was to let her know he wasn't making a dig at her for her fake one.

"I have enough money in that suitcase to charter a

small plane. The only thing that would have to be filed is a flight plan. The pilot would have our fake names, but they wouldn't be given to the tower unless the plane went down. He would be able to say he had two passengers, one male, one female."

"But I don't have a fake name." Graham shook his head.

"I'll call you Ralph. The pilot won't care who we are as long as he gets paid."

"Okay then. I agree. The faster we get to New York the better. We just need to leave the car for Sam and take a cab to the airport."

"And get a phone." She smiled and added, "And hope the legislature isn't in session and she's at home."

"Well, Albany isn't too far from the house. Either way, we'll find her."

They left the library and were soon in possession of a new phone with Internet access and no way to be traced as they paid cash for a burner.

Parking the car by Sears with Graham's old phone tucked under the seat, they took out her suitcase and re-turned to the mall entrance.

A quick call for a cab to the airport and before she knew it, she'd hired a small plane to take them to New York. She had to pay extra in case the pilot didn't pick up a return fare, but it didn't matter. They needed to get to Graham's sister and see if she could pull some strings to start an investigation into Olivia's mother's attempted murder. Because Olivia knew it was no accident. And even though she knew the pilot was full of hogwash as they say in her adopted state, he would get a return fare. Of the thousands of people who flew from LaGuardia each day, one had to be coming this way.

But she paid his fee with no questions. If she didn't balk or act like a jackass, chances of him remembering this fare as anything out of the ordinary were slimmer. In case anyone followed Sam to get the SUV and got curious about where they'd gone from here.

Graham sat in one of the beige leather seats and ran his palms over the hand-rests. "I have to say, this is much nicer than the army transports I've been in."

She laughed. "I should hope so. This isn't a pleasure trip, but it's at least not a combat plane."

"Make no mistake, Olivia. This *is* combat, and we're on a mission. Don't let plush surroundings make you soft. That's the fastest way to get dead."

He was right. After they eluded those men with the help of the hay baler, she'd grown lax and less vigilant. She needed to remember. This was no game. Not at all.

⁂

The plane trip went much too fast for Graham's liking. He really didn't relish seeing his sister and asking for a favor. She'd turned her back on him before, and he hadn't ever made any requests of her again.

True, this time it wasn't for him but for someone else. A someone who had plenty of money. Money that could be donated to the senator for her next campaign.

The uncharitable thought took hold and grew roots.

Yes, that would be how he could play it. Make the request on Olivia's behalf as a constituent. Better yet, let Olivia make it herself. Promise the greedy senator a big check. That would work. Lord knew the lady had no human compassion in her heart. It was all dollars, power and the limelight for her now.

Back at the library when he looked at her picture, his heart contracted hard for what they'd lost. She was his older sister, and it still hurt to know she hadn't cared enough about him to lift one finger to help him.

He also missed his nephews. They were practically grown now based on that photo. He hated to have been left out of their lives, but he couldn't seem to get past her inaction in his desperate time of need.

Olivia, seated facing him, nudged his knee. "What are you thinking about so intently over there? The scowl on your face is enough to terrify small animals."

"Planning how to approach the senator."

"You can't even call her by her name?"

"I can, but I prefer not to. To all intents and purposes, Lisa is gone. She's not the same girl I grew up with."

"Wow. That's some statement." She tilted her head and looked at him for a few moments. Finally, she said, "I can't pretend to understand as I'm an only child. But I also can't fathom, if I were lucky enough to have a sibling, what could happen that would make me never want to contact that person again."

"It's a long story." Graham ran a hand over his hair, pulling some of it out of the rubber band.

He really didn't want to go into it, but Olivia deserved at least a taste of what they'd be dealing with.

"We have time." She leaned forward and lightly touched his leg. "I imagine whatever it was broke your heart because, as you know, I've figured out you aren't really the persona you've put on for Lord knows how many years. You're way more sensitive than you allow people to know."

"Let's keep that between us. I can't afford to lose my street cred."

"And now you're doing that thing you always do with changing the subject when something hits too close to personal."

"Hanging out with you is dangerous in more ways than one."

She smiled. "Why's that?"

"You worm your way into a guy's mind, and all the illusions he thinks he's mastered are stripped away."

"Yeah, I'm good like that." Olivia sat back in her seat. "Seriously, you don't have to share if you don't want to, but I'd like to know what I'm getting myself into. I met Lisa Matthews once or twice when she was a freshman in the New York House of Representatives. As I recall, she was young—the youngest ever elected, by the way—and eager to help. Almost too avid, if you know what I mean."

"Yes, I do. And it only got worse as she moved up. That's the whole *I wasn't popular in school, and now I'm going to make everyone regret the way they treated me* thing. She had these big plans to get so powerful that when the ones who were mean to her as she grew up needed something, she could say no. Either that or charge them exorbitant fees in the guise of donations."

"Really? That's horrific."

"And that's my sister. She's great at putting on a façade of kindness and well-meaning gestures but when the knife comes out, watch out."

"Dare I presume she did something like that to you?"

"Something much worse but you get the idea." Graham didn't want to get into a conversation about his capture and torture and how his own sister, the senator from New York, was one of the holdouts on the vote by the National Security Council to mount a rescue operation for him and his men.

When he *did* get home safely, scarred and unable to walk, she confessed she thought he'd never find out about it. She figured he'd die and never be the wiser.

That really hurt. That his sister wanted him dead. Or, even if what she said about not wanting to appear biased in the voting since her own brother was one of the prisoners was true, how she could leave him to that fate was mind-boggling. Her own little brother. He couldn't begin to fathom it. No man should be left behind, related or not. He'd lost all respect for her when he learned the news. No matter that she'd tried to make it up to him. There was no going back on that. Too much death and destruction of lives happened because her no vote kept the rescue operation from happening as soon as it should have.

"Wow. I don't even know the story, and I feel like apologizing for your offer to ask her to help me. How much do you think it's going to cost?"

"I don't know but be prepared to offer a hefty donation to her campaign war chest or maybe even finance a remodel of her office." He barked out a laugh. "Be warned as well, I don't know how she will receive me. She could put on the queenly persona where she's deigning to entertain the people beneath her or she could put on the concerned sister, *oh my poor dear brother*, act. One never knows who they will get when they ask to see Senator Matthews."

"You really despise her, don't you?"

Olivia had no idea. He loved his sister so much, but after all she'd done to him, he couldn't let himself. He had to keep up the wall.

"I guess you could say that." Graham looked out the window. "I see land out there now. We must be descending."

She leaned toward her own window. "You're right. I see the Hudson River, I think."

"Then it's almost show time. You ready?"

"I think so. Are we going straight to her house?"

"Yep. Better to meet the lion in her lair than wait for her to come to us because that would never happen. Mere mortals don't call her to come visit them. Mere mortals must bow at her throne."

"And maybe even kiss her ring?"

"Oh no, my dear, you must *buy* her ring."

The plane landed on the tarmac with a thud and a screech of tires.

Graham's stomach tightened. Much as he hated it, he'd soon be face to face with his sister.

Chapter 12

Watching Graham's face as the plane landed, Olivia came very close to calling off the whole thing with his sister. It was obvious there was some real issue there and knowing the man as she did now that she'd spent all this time with him, he wasn't making up some story to scare her. He really had deep-seated resentment toward the senator and Olivia was afraid he could lose it in the upcoming confrontation with his sibling.

Not that she thought he'd hurt Senator Matthews. She sensed some part of him would be sacrificed in asking the lady for assistance. Olivia didn't mind paying the senator for her help, but something in the way Graham acted led her to believe this was a huge mistake.

Soon enough though, they had a car and found themselves in the driveway of a large estate off the Long Island Expressway.

Graham rolled down the window and pressed the intercom button on one of the brick pilasters that held up a massive iron gate they would need to pass through.

"Yes?" a disembodied voice came from the speaker beside the button.

"It's Graham Rockford. Here to see Lisa Matthews."

"One moment, sir."

After what seemed like an hour but was more like ten minutes, the voice came back. "I'm sorry. The senator isn't entertaining at the moment."

"This isn't entertainment. I'm her brother. Let her know I'm here and need to see her."

"I am aware of who you are. I am merely relaying the message."

"Then go back and tell her I am going to sit here until she agrees to see me."

"She will instruct me to call law enforcement."

"That would be great. Be sure to do that. I'm positive that would attract the media and, when I get the chance to tell them the illustrious senator won't even open the gates to her combat-wounded brother, they will have some nice articles for the evening news and the late papers."

"One moment, sir." Olivia wasn't sure, but it sounded as if the man on the other end of the phone was having a hard time not laughing.

"Combat wounded?" she asked.

"I didn't get these scars in a bar fight."

"Another taboo subject?"

Before he could respond, the gates swung inward and Graham drove up toward the house.

And what a house. It was magnificent. Large, Italianate and probably gaudy inside. It was obviously a very expensive dwelling but completely not to Olivia's taste.

"You grew up here?"

"Part of the time. We also had a home in Manhattan."

"So we're not so different then. We had a Hamptons house and a penthouse in town."

"I bet you didn't go to military school, though." He shot her an incomprehensible look as he brought the car to a stop in front of the marble staircase.

"No. I didn't."

"My dad was determined to make a man of me, as they say."

"But at the cost of not much time with your family?"

"Exactly. Which probably explains a lot about the dynamics between me and my sister."

Olivia opened her door and placed a foot on the ground. "I can't say that I'm looking forward to meeting her. And now that I'm here, I wish we'd gone to a hotel first and taken showers. We're still in the same ratty clothes."

"You're right." He got out on his side. "We should've saved this visit for tomorrow morning. It's right at dinnertime for her—or this used to be the time she ate—so she's probably in a snit that we interrupted her meal."

They stepped onto the porch. Graham knocked once.

The man who answered must have been standing there waiting for them since there was no hesitation in the opening of the door. "Come in. The senator will see you in the drawing room."

The man led the way to a room on the left. Olivia gave it the once-over. Yes, this was truly a showplace, but it was as if the senator believed that if an item sat still, it needed to be gilded. The whole thing made for an ostentatious show of no taste. She repressed a shudder.

When they were alone, Olivia asked, "Was this the décor when you lived here?"

"Not quite so much but a variation of it." Graham ran his hand across the top of the grand piano. He had a wistful look on his face, but before she could ask, a woman Olivia recognized as the senator entered the room.

"Graham. How very like you to arrive unannounced and at dinnertime. I'm sorry to say we have company and there's no place for you." A sly smile came over her face. "Or, maybe you could play for your supper. You *do* still play, don't you?" She nodded at the piano.

"Of course. And better than you can ever hope to."

"No need to be snide."

"Like your comments weren't?" he asked.

"Why must we always prattle on like children?" The senator seemed to notice Olivia for the first time. "And who have we here? Come on out of the shadows, dear, and let me see who my prodigal brother has dragged home this time."

Already not liking the woman for the way she talked down to her sibling, Olivia stepped forward and glared her displeasure at her.

The senator let out a gasp. Olivia wasn't sure if it was because she recognized her or because of the state of her attire but she soon got her answer.

"My dear brother, I had no idea you knew the runaway heiress. How ever did you meet her?" Senator Matthews put her hand to her brow. "Oh yes, she was discovered in a ratty old bar in that same backwoods town you found refuge in when you ran away yourself. How remiss of me to forget."

Olivia wanted to smack the smug look off the lady's face and call her to task about the way she treated her brother, to say nothing of the trash talk about her bar and the only place that seemed like home. She knew she shouldn't if she expected to have this woman help her get an investigation launched.

"That's enough, Lisa. We're here to ask for your assistance in your official capacity." Graham came to stand beside Olivia. He took hold of her hand. She couldn't help but think it was to restrain her. How he knew she wanted to wipe that superior look off Lisa Matthews' face, she didn't have a clue. She had a good idea he wanted to do the same thing.

"You should call my office for an appointment then." The senator focused on Olivia. "It is nice to see you back in New York. Will you be opening the Hamptons house again? When I saw your stepfather the other day, he was bemoaning the fact that it had been empty for a while except for the staff. He was mentioning how much your mother always liked coming out to see you there."

"He is *not* my stepfather."

"Well, of course, he is, dear. He's married to your mother."

Graham squeezed Olivia's hand.

Before she could respond to the comment about her mother's husband, the senator went on, "He was so glad when you surfaced, he sent Bradford to fetch you. I imagine he won't be pleased you turned up with my brother instead, but I know he'll be thrilled to have you home no matter how you got here." She snapped her fingers. "Oh, you know what? I'm having a fundraiser tomorrow night. I'll give Bradford a call to bring you as his date. I imagine you'll start planning the wedding now that you've seen sense and come back. Running a raunchy little bar isn't very ladylike, is it?"

"Let's go." Olivia pulled on Graham's hand. "We've wasted our time here." She dragged him toward the front door.

"*Your* time? What about my time?" His sister was right on their heels. "I'm a New York senator, and you barged into my home threatening to go to the press if I didn't see my pitiful brother, and now you dismiss me and say I've wasted *your* time? We'll see about that."

The woman was a lunatic. One second she was trying to woo Olivia and the next, she was practically screeching at her.

This was one seriously messed up lady. No wonder Graham didn't want to come to her for help. And it was quite obvious whose side the senator was on.

Time to come up with another plan. But first Olivia was going to get a hotel room, a shower, and some food. In that order.

❧❧❧

In the car, Graham turned to Olivia. "See? She's a loose cannon."

"You're the master of the understatement there, mister. Get me out of here and to a hotel. One with a massive tub I can soak in for hours."

"To get the road dirt off?"

"That and the icky muck I feel like I swam in at the senator's house." She reached over and squeezed his hand. "I'm so sorry. I'd never have asked you to bring me here if I'd known how truly awful she is."

"It was my idea. Don't beat yourself up. I knew better but was hoping to help you. I thought I could put my own animosity behind me for that purpose." He turned the car to head out the gates.

"You did. You were actually wonderful. She was the one full of vinegar."

"Thanks. I tried." He thought about his sister and her mean words. Why was she being so awful? If anyone had the right to be hateful, it was him. After all, he was the one who was tortured, not her. Maybe it was the guilt of leaving him there to his fate? He didn't know. Not being a psychiatrist, he couldn't begin to understand the woman. What he did know, though, was that he'd never approach her again. She was toxic to him, and he didn't need that in his life.

"We need a plan B now," he said.

"We can worry about that tomorrow. Right now, shower."

"I thought you wanted a bath."

"The way I feel, I'll do both."

"Good enough." He nodded. "Where will we stay? I'm sure the senator has already made her call to let the world know we're in town."

"You still have the Glock, right?"

"Of course."

"Then we head straight into Manhattan and stay at the Marriott Marquis. Anyone messes with us, they can meet Mr. Glock and tell him their story. Heck, we might stop at a hardware store and get me another Stillson."

"Now you're talking. Let's meet them head on." He turned the car toward the Manhattan skyline and passed her the burner phone. "Call and get us a room."

"I'm on it."

Traffic was light, so they made it to the Marriott quickly. Graham pulled the car into the valet area and told them the luggage was in the trunk. He'd put the clothes he bought at the mall into her suitcase, so there was just the one between them.

They rode the elevator up to the lobby, and she registered them under her real name. He admired her for that. It seemed the meeting with his sister had served one purpose. Olivia Jacobs was done hiding.

He'd known she was gutsy when she whacked those punks with her wrench but this was a whole new level. Going out in the open after hiding for years took nerve and moxie. And it suddenly dawned on him that he was falling hard for the lady.

Pushing that thought aside as well as thoughts of Clara that suddenly surfaced, he pasted a smile on his face as Olivia came over where he waited. "I got two keys, even though I'm not comfortable being alone in the room by myself, so, even though I'm giving you one, you can't use it."

"You've got nothing to worry about. I don't plan to let you out of my sight, except for the time you spend in that bath you want so desperately."

"Then let's get to it." She turned toward the bank of elevators with him right behind her, keeping an eye out in case they'd been followed. No sense in taking chances now that it was known that Olivia was in New York.

Inside their room, Graham was slightly disappointed that she'd gotten a room with two beds rather than a king room. Why he'd think she'd want to share a bed with him again, he didn't know. It still stung a little any way.

"You go ahead and get in the shower, and I'll call out and order something for dinner," he said.

"No. Don't."

"We have to eat. I don't know about you, but I'm a growing boy."

"I just don't want you going out without me. If you go to pick up food, I'll be alone."

"How about room service then?"

"How will we know if the person delivering the food is really a hotel employee?"

Now she was getting ridiculous. He could understand being careful, but he really didn't relish the thought of not having dinner.

"There's a peephole in the door, and I can answer with my weapon in hand. Might scare the guy to death but we'd at least have something to eat."

"Oh, good grief then. Order a burger for me. With fries." She opened the suitcase she'd set on the bed. Pulling out a change of clothes, she turned to the bathroom. "See you when my skin is wrinkled from being in the water too long."

"What if your burger gets cold?"

"Then I eat it cold." She grinned and disappeared behind the door.

When Graham heard the water running, he picked up the receiver and called down for two burgers, fries and a couple of beers.

He liked a woman with an appetite. None of those skinny salad-nibbling girls for him. There was almost nothing he hated worse than a woman sitting across a table from him with a look of hunger on her face as she ate grass and he ate a steak.

Olivia was true to her word. She stayed in the bath for a long time. He turned on the late news and waited for their food to arrive.

He was able to open the door and allow the waiter to push the laden cart into the room without incident. As soon as the man was gone, Graham knocked on the door to the bathroom. "Dinner time."

She came out in a pair of red flannel pajamas with penguins on them. Her hair was wet and hung straight. "Ahh. I feel so much better now. That was just what I needed."

"Cute outfit," he said.

She turned around as if in a fashion show. "You think so?"

"It's not sexy lingerie, but somehow, it suits you."

"Thanks." She paused then added, "I think." Olivia walked over to the table and lifted the silver dome from one of the plates. "Gosh, that looks good."

"Then dig in." He held the chair out for her, and she sat.

Taking the seat opposite her, he said, "I saw a news story about your mother's husband."

"What was it?"

"It seems he's the host of the fundraiser tomorrow for my sister's campaign."

"Good Lord, we almost asked the exact wrong person to help us, didn't we?"

"For sure. But now we know who to go to."

She took a bite of her burger. Once she swallowed, she asked, "Who?"

"The opposition." Graham winked. "I happen to know someone who can get us an audience with him."

"But will he see you once he knows she's your sister? Why would he trust anything we said?"

"Because the guy I know who can get us in happens to be someone who was in my unit in Baghdad. *That* man trusts me with his life and knows I wouldn't pull any kind of stunt. He'll convince our man that we're on the up and up."

"You were in Baghdad?"

"I was." He hoped she wouldn't push him for details.

After a long moment where she stared at him, and he remained silent, she eventually shrugged and focused on her burger.

Relieved not to have to go into details at the moment although he knew he'd eventually have to talk to her about his wounds, Graham ate his own dinner.

Their silence was accompanied by the sound of the television and the traffic out in Times Square.

Chapter 13

The next morning, almost as soon as it was light, Olivia rolled over and glanced at the clock. Too early to get up. She could hear Graham's deep breathing from the bed where he slept. Wanting to make sure he got plenty of rest since she'd been keeping him going on high alert for too many days in a row, she stayed quiet and thought over what needed to be done next.

Knowing he was going to try to set up a meeting with his sister's opposition in the senate race, she also wanted to speak to him about accompanying her to see her lawyer. She'd been transacting business with him in a roundabout way for a long time and wanted to see the man face to face while she was in town.

She wasn't fooled for one second that she was safe and didn't want to let her guard down. The need to survive to age thirty was still vital so she could change her beneficiary. If this plan to expose her mother's husband came to nothing, she knew she'd have to disappear again.

A visit to her lawyer while she could get one in sounded like a good idea to her.

"I don't know what you're thinking about so hard over there, but you need to ease off before your brain explodes." Graham's voice startled her.

"I thought you were asleep."

"You woke me up with all that concentrating." He sat up with the covers bunched at his waist. At some time in the night, he'd taken off his shirt. Now not only did his stomach muscles contract as he stretched his arms, but his scars glistened in the dawn's light. The man was fit, that was for sure. Probably from all that work at his ranch as he didn't seem the gym rat type. She wished he'd trust her with his real story.

"Sorry. In the future, I'll try to concentrate quieter."

"Good." He nodded. "Now's my turn in the shower. Do you need to use the facilities before I hop in?"

"Thanks for asking. Yes." She rose and made her way to the bathroom. Once inside she leaned against the sink and hoped he'd cover himself before she went back in the other room. He was too darn sexy for comfort. She couldn't afford to get distracted by a cute smile, mussed hair and a hot, albeit scarred, body.

When she had control of herself, she stepped back into the main room. "All yours."

He was still in his boxers and nothing else.

She averted her eyes as he limped into the bathing area carrying his clean clothes. She'd forgotten again how his left leg was shorter than his right. It truly wasn't noticeable when he had on his boots.

Wishing she knew what happened to him, she turned on the morning news to pass the time while he showered.

Taking advantage of Graham being out of the room, Olivia changed into a pair of jeans and a pullover sweater. She found a pair of socks in the suitcase and was ready to go as soon as Graham was. Except for brushing her teeth.

There was nothing exciting on the news, so she turned it off.

The door to the bathroom opened. "I'm thinking we call my friend this morning and set a time to chat with him as soon as he's available."

"I'd also like to call my lawyer and go by to see him while I'm in town."

"I'm not sure that's a good idea."

"Why not? I trust him. He's known where I've been all this time—well, sort of—and has never betrayed me."

"I didn't mean that. What I meant was that I think it would be a mistake to go to his office. You'd be in too much danger. If, on the other hand, you wanted to set a place outside his office to meet, we could probably do that. I'd be sure to have you under surveillance. Be ready for anything."

"Anything?"

"Within reason, of course." He pointed to her chest.

She looked down. Did the sweater have a stain? "What?"

"News flash. We're not in Texas anymore. You need something warmer than that." He pointed to his own chest. "See. I've got a sweatshirt."

"I didn't pack a jacket. I guess that's on the agenda now, too."

"Somehow, I think we can find a store here."

She smiled despite herself. "You think?"

They were headed out on serious errands, and she knew him well enough by now to know he was joking around to ease the stress. How she hadn't seen that humor was the way he dealt with things before now was a mystery. He'd been doing it almost since the moment she met him.

Graham held his arm out. "Come along then."

She tucked her hand into the crook of his elbow. "Lead on."

"Let's eat breakfast at Junior's." He inclined his head toward the restaurant across the street.

"You eat more than anyone I know."

"Three meals a day is all." He scratched his head. "And maybe a snack or two once in a while."

After they ordered, Graham pulled out the burner phone and made his call. Once he was done, he passed it to her. "I think a good place to meet your lawyer would be at the skating rink at Rockefeller Center."

"That's pretty public, isn't it?"

"Exactly."

"How can you protect me in that mass of people?"

"Easy. We seat you at one of the tables right inside overlooking the rink. There are a few in the corners that would be perfect. Open on three sides. Where we can see anyone coming."

"Wouldn't it be better to be closed in?"

"Nope. Trust me on this. You want to see them before they're on you."

Somehow Olivia sensed they were no longer talking about the people who were after her. The emotion coming off Graham in waves was rawer than that. More like personal demons of his own.

She nodded, hoping he would continue.

When he didn't, she made her own call.

Their food was served as she spoke with her lawyer and arranged the meet-up for that afternoon.

The breakfast was good, and once they paid, they strolled down toward the Levi's store. She bought a jacket and put it on immediately.

"Now I'm ready to conquer the day. This is cozy." She laughed at herself. "I never thought I'd be so happy about a fifty dollar coat."

"I'm glad being warm makes you happy." Graham held the door open. "It's almost time to meet my guy. We need to take a cab to Columbus Circle. His office is across the street from Central Park."

She stepped onto the sidewalk then moved back in so fast, she collided with Graham's chest.

"What happened? Did you trip?"

Grabbing his hand, she tugged him behind a mannequin. "It's Bernard. Outside."

"Bernard?"

"My mother's husband. He's standing across the road. Out there. Oh my God."

❧❧❧

Graham couldn't believe it. He'd led her right into danger. After all they'd been through, he'd screwed up. Royally. They should have stayed the hell out of New York. His sister was never going to help them, and he'd been a fool to think she would. He should've kept Olivia in some hidey-hole until he could get the man who tried to kill her mother arrested. He shouldn't have allowed Olivia to register at the Marriott under her own name. What arrogance they'd had. To think they could walk into town and announce themselves and still be safe. Stupid, stupid, stupid.

Glancing around to try to figure out what to do, he spied another door. "Come on. We've not lost yet." He pulled Olivia toward the back of the store. "Pretend to be sick," he whispered as they approached the sales clerk.

She bent over almost double and let out a moan. "I'm sorry. My wife is ill. I think she might be having a miscarriage. Can we use the side exit?"

"I'm not supposed to open it," the young man said. He peered at Olivia. "She looks terrible."

"I know, and I'm afraid to take her out there with all the crowds. They're relentless, and she doesn't have the energy to deal with the mass of people out there."

Olivia moaned again.

"Okay. Okay." The clerk led them to the door. "Just don't tell my boss."

Once they were outside, Graham said, "Can you run? Let's get on Eighth Avenue as quick as we can and then hail a cab. Hopefully, they aren't watching this area all the way to Eighth."

"I say we go for it. We've got nothing to lose."

"There's a Chinese place at the corner. Run there and wait for me if you get there ahead of me."

"What are you going to do? We both know you can probably move way faster than I can."

"I doubt that." Didn't she remember he had a gimp leg? He guessed it was good that she didn't recall his handicap, but it also made for a weird sensation of someone thinking he was a whole man again. He didn't quite know how to process that.

No time for those thoughts now. Time to run. Or lope, depending on who you are. "I'm not planning on any heroics, Olivia. I just plan to stay behind you with my weapon ready in case I need to use it."

"Please tell me you aren't going to run down the street in Manhattan shooting as if we're in the Wild West."

"Only if I need to." He pressed his hand on her bottom. "Go. I'm right behind you."

As soon as they started running, Graham realized he'd never asked her what this Bernard guy looked like. How dumb was that?

She ran ahead of him and being slim and agile, she was able to negotiate her way past all the people quickly. He followed at a more sedate pace. Seeing no one approach her, he still kept alert and one hand on his weapon.

In a few moments, he caught up to her on the corner by the Chinese place. "Made it so far."

"Let's catch that cab."

Graham stepped out and whistled for a passing taxi.

They settled in, and as the driver took off, Olivia squeezed his thigh. "Look, right there. It's him."

Graham glanced out the window, memorizing the face and body size of the man on the sidewalk. Bernard had dark hair touched with silver, was tall, dignified, and dressed in an expensive cashmere coat.

Now Graham had his enemy in his head and would never forget him.

"We barely made it." Olivia's face reflected the horror she had to be feeling.

"But we did, and now we move forward, right?"

"Yes. Moving on. Not looking back."

Graham hoped she was right and that they *could* move on. He didn't think the man would've done anything to her on the crowded street, but he'd shown how persistent he could be. Knowing Bernard wasn't going to give up merely strengthened Graham's own resolve.

This woman beside him in the cab was going to survive even if he had to die to make it happen. Hopefully, it wouldn't come to that, but he was ready to take that step if necessary. Evil couldn't win out.

It took the taxi fifteen minutes to make it to Columbus Circle. Traffic was dense, but it always was as he recalled from when he lived in town.

Once they paid the fare, Graham led Olivia into the building that housed a shopping mall as well as offices. His army pal was going to meet them at the door to the suite that housed the headquarters to the man running against Lisa. Graham wanted to be sure to have his ally there in case the candidate doubted his sincerity since he was related to the opposition.

They stepped off the elevator to find Graham's friend pacing the area in front of them. "Hey, Rockford. Long time, no see."

"For sure, Roberts. Been too long. We need to go for a beer later."

"No can do, man. I've given up the evil beverage. Got me a reckless driving offense and promised not to touch the stuff again."

"Good for you to keep it up."

"Who's the pretty lady?"

"This is my friend, Olivia Jacobs. She's the one who needs to see your man."

"Since she's such a looker, I'm sure he'll want to help her." He turned and walked down the corridor.

Graham knew the comment about her looks wasn't going to go over well with Olivia and hoped she wouldn't voice her displeasure. He cast a glance in her direction and even though she looked like she would burst, she kept quiet. Sure he'd get an earful later, he cupped his hand around her elbow and led her toward the door Roberts opened.

Entering the pale blue painted room, they were faced with a receptionist holding a phone to her ear. She indicated for them to take a seat.

When the receptionist hung up, she smiled at them. "Let me buzz the boss and let him know you're here."

"Thanks," Graham said.

In a few moments, the door to an inner office

opened, and a large man with a handlebar mustache stepped out. His face was florid, and he looked like a heart attack waiting to happen.

"Come in, come in. I recognize you, of course, Miss Jacobs. And I understand you're the brother of my worthy adversary." The candidate held out his hand. "Jonathan Hofstra at your service."

Graham and Olivia shook his hand, and once they were ensconced in his slightly darker painted office, he said, "To what do I owe this visit? I must say it seems most unorthodox."

"That's why I wanted Roberts here. To vouch for us. We need your help, and I want you to be assured there's no ulterior motive that would assist my sister's campaign."

"I'll admit, I'm a bit concerned about that. I know she never says anything about her extended family in her ads or propaganda, but I'm a bit leery when a brother of an adversary turns up on my doorstep so to speak."

"It's really for me that Graham is here. May I explain?" Olivia asked.

"Sure. Sure, Miss Jacobs. I'd love to offer my assistance to one of the Jacobs family if it's within my powers to do so." He leaned back in his chair and placed his hands behind his head. "Regale me with your tale."

Chapter 14

Not sure exactly where to start, Olivia sat for a moment to gather her thoughts. She wanted to trust this Hofstra man but wasn't sure if he was someone to put her faith in. He seemed way too much of a political glad-hander to be of much assistance.

Finally deciding she really didn't have much of a choice, she took a deep breath and started to talk.

"As you obviously know who I am, I presume you also know my mother has been in a coma for almost six years now."

"Yes. I know. Tragic event. Tragic. As I recall, she was a beautiful woman."

"She still is. As far as I know, that is. I haven't seen her, but I hear she's getting first-rate care in the facility being paid for by her trust fund."

"Her husband isn't paying for that?" Hofstra scratched his head. "Seems like I heard he was bragging about the amounts of money he'd been shelling out to keep her alive for years."

"He's a liar. It hasn't cost him one cent. My father settled a lot of money on my mother when they divorced. He never stopped loving her, but she wanted out. Making sure she never wanted for anything again was paramount for Dad."

"And you're sure this money still exists?"

"Yes. Positive. My father made me her beneficiary. Irrevocable." Olivia ran her suddenly sweaty palms on the thighs of her jeans. "I've made sure the bill is paid every month."

"Does the husband have access to the funds?" Hofstra asked.

"Only the interest. The principal is protected unless the trustees see a need to invade it. It's my understanding that the principal has been invaded on a few occasions. Once to pay for some renovations to the brownstone that's owned by the trust. One other time for some other repairs there and I'm not sure about anything else. I *do* know Bernard has put some pressure on the trustees to give him cash, ostensibly to take care of my mother but really for his own purposes."

"And while you've been gone—I hesitate to say missing since it seems to me the more you talk, the more I think you've been hiding—you've been in touch with these trustees?"

"Not directly but I have a lawyer who keeps an eye on things for me, and I receive reports periodically."

Hofstra leaned forward, elbows on the table. "And what do you think I can do for you in regard to this? Where is this conversation going?"

Graham made a sound as if he were going to speak. Olivia held her hand out to signal him that she had it under control.

"It's in Bernard's interests to keep my mother alive but to have me gone."

"What do you mean by *gone*, young lady?"

"Gone as in dead."

Hofstra sat back in his chair. "Why would that benefit him? And what can I do about it?"

"Right now, my mother is my beneficiary and I'm hers. I can't change mine until I'm thirty. Two years from now. If I die before that time, my share goes to her trust and her estate. Then, Bernard is her heir as far as I know."

"As far as you know?"

"Yeah. Before she got sick, we talked and she said she'd just finished updating her will to have all funds go to Bernard if I predeceased her. The next thing I knew, she was in a coma. A perfectly healthy lady with no issues was suddenly bedridden and uncommunicative."

"And you think her husband is responsible?" Hofstra leaned forward again. Eagerness shone on his face. She didn't like the avidness expressed there, but if she was going to get him to help her, she'd have to live with it. It was almost as if he sniffed blood in the water and a bad outcome for his opponent since Lisa Matthews's campaign was tied to Bernard.

"I'm positive. Almost as soon as my mother lapsed into the coma, things started happening to me. Like accidents designed to take me out."

"Really? What do you think he did to your mother?"

"I don't know. Some kind of injections. To make her sick."

"Did you call the police and tell them of your suspicions?" Hofstra rubbed his chin as if thinking over everything Olivia said.

"Yes, but nothing happened. I'm not sure if he bribed the officer in charge or if they merely discounted what I said since I was so young. All I know is law enforcement did nothing. That's when I decided I needed to disappear."

"And you stayed successfully hidden until you whacked those idiots in your bar." Hofstra clapped his hands. "Well done."

"But now I've been discovered, and I want Bernard's activities investigated. It's the only way I can stay safe without disappearing again."

"And what do you think I can offer?"

"You have clout in this city. I'd merely like you to do what you can to help get an investigation started. A real investigation, not the farce that happened before."

"While I *do* have clout as you say, what makes you feel I can do any good at all?"

"I don't know if you can. To be honest, we came to New York to see if Senator Matthews could help but learned she and Bernard are actually cohorts." Olivia reached over to Graham and patted his leg. "This man, even though he and his sister have been estranged for years, brought me to her to try to get me some assistance.

For his trouble, he was insulted and tossed out of her home."

"Really? That makes me very curious. Why does this sister of yours hate you?" Hofstra asked Graham.

"It's a long story. Suffice it to say I don't plan to visit her again. Ever." Graham covered Olivia's hand with his.

"I'll need some time to figure this out. Can you come back this evening?"

"No. I'm afraid not. We need to keep moving. I know my sister has a fund-raising event tonight. We'd like to have something happening before that occurs. We have some other people to see as well." Graham stood. "Thanks for your time."

"Wait one minute." Hofstra stood as well. "I want an exclusive on this."

"If you're not even willing to say you'll make one phone call for us, why should we give you the exclusive rights to break a story if there's an investigation?" Graham asked.

"I'll make a call. Please wait out in the lobby, and I'll be out in a few minutes."

"We'll wait ten minutes. Then we're gone." Graham led the way out. He kept going until they were in front of the elevators. Without pressing a button, he looked at her. "I'm sorry, but we can't afford to stand around for long. We really don't know who he's calling. For all we know, he's pals with Bernard as well."

"You're right. I'm not sure about him at all. I see him as someone who plays both sides of the game, depending on who is ahead at the time." She paced back and forth then stopped. "I'm having a panic attack. Let's go. I don't feel safe."

He grabbed her hand. "I still have my gun. Let's wait him out."

"I can't." Olivia panted, trying to catch her breath. All she needed now was to hyperventilate. Trying to gain control of herself and settle down, she placed her right palm on the wall and bent over, making an effort to get calm.

"Come on then. I don't want you to pass out. We'll get you somewhere you feel safer and then I'll contact Hofstra from there."

She nodded. "Yes. Let's get out of here. It's like a trap."

Graham pressed the elevator button, and when the doors opened, Olivia was relieved to see no one inside.

They boarded and rode down to the bottom floor.

At the door to the street, Roberts came running up beside them. "Where are you going? Hofstra sent me to get you, and I saw the doors of the elevator shut with you on board."

"We decided to go on to our next appointment so we wouldn't be late," Olivia said.

"Hofstra is off the phone. He wants to see you. Can you move your appointment to a later time?" Roberts asked.

"No. We need to be on the move." Graham held his hand out to Roberts. "Thanks for your help, man. I'll check in later with Hofstra. We're grateful for his help, but we have to go."

"He's not going to be happy." Roberts was almost pouting.

"Have no fear, we won't be blabbing to the public about our plans. If he can get an investigation started, he's welcome to set up a press conference, and we'll come for that. I'll call later and see if he's got one arranged."

"I guess he'll have to be happy with that."

"He sure will because we aren't going back up right now," Olivia said. She pushed on the glass door and walked out, followed by Graham.

Roberts was right behind them. "Rockford, come back. You know you owe me."

Graham spun around so fast, Olivia almost lost her balance as he brushed against her.

"I wondered when that would come up." Graham practically snarled the words.

Roberts held his hands up. "I didn't want to play that card, but you gave me no choice."

"There's always a choice." Graham glanced over at Olivia then back at Roberts. "If I didn't want to help this lady so badly, I would tell you *and* Hofstra where to go and even buy you a first class ticket from the devil. But since I am so concerned about her, I am going to put my personal animosity aside and forgive you for that low blow."

"I'm sorry I had to say it."

"No. I don't think you are." Graham turned to Olivia.

"Let's get out of here. I should've listened to you sooner. Your gut instincts are spot on." He stepped out and hailed a cab.

As soon as they were seated in the back of the taxi, she said, "What was that all about?"

He was still fuming mad. His face was red and scared her as she thought he might actually burst a blood vessel or have a stroke. His breath came in short spurts, and it was a few moments before he could respond.

"Without going into great detail, Roberts was with me when I was injured, and he dragged me to safety." Graham wiped his brow with a shaking hand. "Apparently, that means I have to do whatever he tells me. I'm stunned that a soldier would exact such a price for doing his duty in uniform."

"Wow. That is crazy. It smacks of that old tradition of *I saved your life, you have to return the favor before you're released from the debt.* That is just wrong. I thought I liked Roberts, but now I'm sure I don't. That was uncalled for."

"You're right about that. I'm so stunned, I can't even think straight."

"We need to go somewhere quiet and have a few moments to regain our equilibrium before we meet with my lawyer," Olivia said. She leaned forward and changed their destination with the cabbie.

The taxi pulled up in front of Serendipity a few minutes later. She smiled at Graham. "I don't know about you, but a frozen hot chocolate always makes me feel better."

"Never tried it but it couldn't hurt."

They paid the fare and got out.

Once they had the massive drink to share, Olivia stretched her hand across the table and touched his. "Will you tell me now about your injury? I feel as if I should know."

He nodded and fiddled with the paper from the straw. "I think you've earned the right."

"So what happened?"

"I don't really like to share what happened in combat zones with non-service personnel since it's hard to make them understand exactly how horrific it is so I'm going to give you a broad outline, not details. I hope that's all right."

"I'll take what you're willing to give." She sipped chocolate from her straw. The rush of sugar was making her feel better already.

"We were in a convoy in Baghdad, and an IED exploded, flipping the vehicle in front of ours. I was driving and was able to turn around without hitting the flipped one, but in the process, with the rate of speed of the spin out, I lost control in the dirt. Our vehicle ended up on its side with my leg caught underneath."

Olivia shuddered, thinking about how painful that had to have been. She remembered how well he drove when that car hit them. She couldn't help but wonder if he'd thought about that time in his life when he was evading that driver on the road back in Texas.

"Roberts was able to get out of the passenger seat, and another man in our unit got out from the back. With great effort, they were able to get me out from under the vehicle. My leg was crushed, and one bone stuck out from the shin."

"Oh, that's terrible. Just awful."

"I needed a couple of surgeries and since the bones were crushed, I had to have metal inserted. That's how my left leg ended up shorter than my right."

"And the scars I saw were from the surgeries?"

Graham nodded. "Yes. But I was lucky. All the guys in the flipped Humvee were killed outright. Roberts and the other man weren't injured."

"Anyone else in the convoy hurt?"

"No. Everyone else survived."

"And the scar on your face?"

"Different event." He got that closed look on his face again, and she knew he was done sharing information for now.

Graham took the last swallow of the drink. "Are you ready to go see your lawyer? I think I'm settled enough now to be a competent bodyguard."

"Should we call Hofstra first?"

"Probably but I know as soon as I do, the burner phone will be no good as I am quite sure he has caller ID."

"Let's call Sam first then and check on your livestock as well as the bar," Olivia said.

"Good idea. I know Sam can be trusted but would like to see if there have been any issues."

"Same here."

He made the call, and once they had updates on the

situation back home, Graham dialed Hofstra's number.

Olivia put her ear near the receiver so she could hear the conversation as it occurred. She wished they were somewhere they could use the speaker, but they weren't.

Hofstra got on the line with alacrity. After Graham identified himself, Hofstra said, "I've got a man high up at One Police Plaza who is mounting an investigation. He's already sent some officers to the facility where Miss Jacobs's mother is and will be having some blood work performed to see what kind of chemicals she has in her system even though they aren't sure that will make any difference at this point. If the initial cause of the coma was something like a poisoning, that would've long ago cleared out."

"How will they do that without a warrant or the consent of her husband?" Graham asked,

"Don't worry about that. It's covered."

Olivia opened her eyes wide and arched her brows. If they were acting without the proper permissions, would the findings be admissible if there were any charges to be filed against Bernard? This needed to be done the right way, and she hoped Graham would say something.

"What do we do if they find some issue? If there's no warrant, how will the results be used against Bernard? In other words, if he did something to her, how will we get to an arrest if we aren't following the law?"

Relieved that Graham asked, Olivia let out the breath she'd been holding.

"I told you, it's covered. We got a judge to sign off on it."

"It's on the up and up? The judge granted a warrant? On what grounds?" Graham pushed the issue with Hofstra.

"I'm telling you, it's all aboveboard and legal. We'll be having a press conference at the same time Senator Matthews is kicking off her soiree tonight. I expect you and Miss Jacobs here thirty minutes before so we can get set up."

"We'll be there if you need us."

"We need *her*. Count on it."

"Then I'll make sure she's there on time." Graham ended the call and turned the phone off. "At least if it's off, maybe it can't be traced."

"Just throw it out of the cab as we head to Rockefeller center."

He laughed. "I *knew* I liked you. That's a brilliant plan."

⌘

Thirty minutes later, Olivia walked to a corner table near the plate glass window where patrons could watch the ice skaters at Rockefeller Center. Her lawyer was already seated and waiting for her.

He stood and gave her a hug. "You look great. It's been too long since we've seen each other."

"I know. You're still as young-looking as you were three years ago when we got to chat in Colorado."

"Thanks." He rubbed his stomach. "Although I think married life has helped me put on about fifteen pounds."

"You wear it well. I hope your wife is doing okay."

"She is. Except for being ready to deliver our first baby any time."

"Congrats. How does it feel to be a first-time father at age fifty?"

"That's what's keeping me young-looking, I guess. I can certainly recommend marrying a younger partner. She definitely keeps me hopping."

"And a little one will add to that for sure."

"I was surprised to find you back in town. As soon as I saw the article about the bar, I figured you'd go to ground, not come back to the city. What's going on?"

"I've gotten some assistance from Jonathan Hofstra. He's got an investigation started into Bernard and my mother's condition. There's a press conference about it at eight tonight. I'll be there."

"Do you think that's wise? Being on the television, I mean. I'm glad about the investigation but should you be in the middle of it?"

"I can't help it. The cost of his assistance was my being involved and willingness to stand and accuse Bernard. I figure that's not too big a price to pay."

"I hope not."

"I have a friend helping me, and he thinks this is the way to go in order to make it where I can spend my life in the open again. You have no idea how much I want to live in safety." Tears welled in her eyes. "It's been really hard. And not one day goes by that I don't worry about my mother."

"I know you love her, even though you and she

didn't always see things the same way. I can't imagine the stress you've been under."

"And I have you to thank for taking care of my business while I've been out of circulation. Thanks for being there and checking on her when you could."

"No problem. I tried to get over there to see how things were with her every two weeks or so. She still looks good, and they are at least taking good care of her."

"Of course they are. If she dies before me, Bernard loses it all. He's got to keep her alive."

"And that leads us to what really worries me about you being here. If you die first, she inherits from you, and then he lets her die. He comes out on top."

"We've known that for years and, sadly, if I hadn't hit those men who tried to rob my bar, I would still be in Texas under the radar. But now I have to deal with the fallout from my own actions. I'm not happy about it at all, but I have to at least give it one more shot. If I fail, I go back into hiding."

"Not to be morbid but that's if you fail *and* survive."

"I have confidence in the man helping me. He's watching us right now, ready to come to my defense if someone approaches."

"That's good, but I hope he doesn't have to act."

"Me, too." She nodded at the folder he had in front of him. "I presume that's some paperwork for my signature."

"You got it. I figured we'd take care of that while I had you here instead of me mailing it to the drop-box for you to retrieve."

"Saved me a road trip." Olivia laughed. "Except that this trip I took was many more miles than I usually have to go."

He opened the folder and slid some documents toward her.

Looking them over, Olivia signed in the areas marked, then stacked them to hand back.

When she glanced up, the blood in her veins froze.

Across the way stood Bernard. Staring straight at her.

She sucked in a breath and whispered, "It's him. Bernard. Right over there."

"Where?"

"Don't look. Pretend all is well. I'm going to walk away and hopefully, Graham will have me covered. I'm sure Bernard won't try anything with this crowd around since he's way more subtle than that, but I'd like to get clear in case he tries to approach."

"No. Stay here. You're safest right here where we are. I'll call for help." He pulled his phone out.

A hand landed on Olivia's shoulder.

Startled, she jumped and let out a little squeal.

"It's me. Relax," Graham said.

"I take it you see Bernard, too?" she asked.

"I do." Graham had a grim look on his face. He addressed her lawyer, "I'm Graham Rockford, and I'm going to ease Olivia out of here. Much as I'd love to stay and chat, I think we need to save that for another day."

"I agree. And I want to apologize as I fear someone may have followed me here. I don't usually leave my office during the day so that odd occurrence may have alerted Bernard or one of his cronies that I was meeting Olivia."

"Too late to worry about that. We've made a lot of mistakes, but as long as we're still breathing, we're still winning."

Olivia stood and backed away from the table. "I'll be in touch."

Graham led her down the hallway farthest from where they'd spotted Bernard. Keeping one hand on her elbow, Graham had the other one on the gun. Well, she presumed so since he had it behind his back.

"Where are we going?"

"Outside and to the street." He kept glancing over his shoulder.

"How do we know Bernard won't try anything out there?"

"We don't, but we couldn't sit inside all day waiting to see what he would do."

"So we go out into a hallway where we can be trapped?"

"No, we go out into a hallway where we can move to the end and walk out to a cab to take us far away," Graham said.

"Maybe we should just turn around and face him. You shoot him if he tries anything."

"Much as I like that plan, I think we need to have him prosecuted if we can rather than taking the law into our own hands. A shoot out at Rockefeller Center could only lead to trouble."

They arrived at the exit. Before Graham could open the door to hustle them out, two elderly women came in.

One walked with a cane, and the other waited for her to pass.

"Olivia," a voice called out behind them as the women ambled past.

Bernard had them trapped. Olivia turned to face the man who ruined her life.

Chapter 15

My dear Olivia, I received a call from my friend, Senator Matthews last night. Imagine my shock when she said you were in the city. Why didn't you let me know you were coming? I'd have had someone meet your plane." Bernard took a step toward them.

Graham moved in front of Olivia to protect her. "Back off."

"I don't believe we've been introduced." Bernard ran his gaze up and down Graham's body with a sneer on his face. "Are you some kind of cowboy?"

"Rancher."

"Bit far from the countryside here, isn't it?"

"I guess so, but that's not important right now, is it?"

"If you'll move aside and let me talk to my step-daughter, I'd be grateful."

"Not happening." Graham adjusted his stance to be more aggressive. "I think if she wanted to chat with you, she'd have let you know. Following her all over Manhattan like you have had made her leery of you and your motives."

"I said step aside, son. You know nothing about Olivia and her obligations to her family. Her mother is ill, and I would hope she wants to visit her."

"I *can* talk, you know," Olivia said as she moved to stand beside Graham.

"Then get rid of the loser and talk to me," Bernard said.

"He's not a loser, and I have nothing to say. Please stop following me and leave me in peace."

"Your mother may be dying. She would want you to visit before she goes. I have a car outside. We can leave from here."

"You *have* lost your mind if you think I am going anywhere with you." Olivia turned to Graham. "Let's go."

"Don't move." Bernard closed the gap between them.

Olivia stepped back at the same moment Graham pushed forward. "Go outside and hail a taxi. I'll hold him here."

"You will do no such thing," Bernard said at the same time Olivia said, "No. I'm not leaving you."

"It appears we're at a stalemate. Won't you just come quietly with me and let's visit your mother and resolve all our issues." Bernard nodded his head, looking at someone or something over Graham's shoulder.

Torn whether to turn to see if there was a person behind him or if Bernard was trying to distract him from protecting Olivia, Graham didn't move for a split second.

Deciding to believe there was no one there, Graham took Olivia's hand tried to push past Bernard. Planning to return to the main area near the skating rink they'd just abandoned, Graham was shocked to find the older man was actually quite fit. He stood firm even when nudged by the side of Graham's body.

Graham pushed again, harder. The older man staggered a few steps, almost losing his footing.

Taking advance of him being off kilter, Graham hustled Olivia down the corridor.

As soon as they were clear of Bernard, Graham said to Olivia, "Walk as fast as you can without making us noticeable. We need to regroup and make a plan. The best way to handle that is back in the crowd."

Rounding the corner, they passed a security guard. "We'd have been better off staying where we were and reporting a stalker to that guy there." Olivia indicated the guard. "That trip down the hall was a waste of time, and now I have no idea how we'll get out of here to get to the press conference."

"I think we have to call Hofstra and ask him to send a car here for us. And to send some bodyguards while he's at it. I can't keep you safe by myself if Bernard has more men around the perimeter of the building."

"Did you see the guy behind me a second ago?" she asked.

"Was there really someone there? I didn't take the time to look."

"He was as big as an ape. Scary."

"Then we definitely need to hire some people to help me keep you safe until the investigation can be done. And much as I hate to say it, we need to leave town and go to ground as soon as the press conference is over."

"I'm thinking we don't need to wait. Let's go now and send for our luggage later."

Graham led Olivia to an empty table with two chairs. He sat facing the direction they'd come from and watched as Bernard and a guy with arm muscles bigger than most men's thighs came to a stop. The two of them stood against the wall and glared at Graham.

"Don't look over there. The goon is with Bernard, and they're clearly set to watch every move you make."

"What's the plan then? We sure can't do anything with them over there," Olivia said.

"I'm calling Hofstra."

"I threw the phone out the window, remember?"

"Yeah, I do, and that's a problem. I haven't seen a public phone in years either so I'm thinking we have to borrow one from some kind soul."

She gave him a grim smile. "Good luck with that in New York."

"You'll be taking that back in a minute. You'll see."

A lady with a baby in a stroller walked close to their table. Graham stood and waved her over. She cast a look in Olivia's direction as if to see if it was safe.

He realized he should've had Olivia try to get her attention. He still forgot about that scar on his face that scared people. Having spent most of his life with a clear complexion, he even startled himself when he caught an accidental glimpse of himself in the mirror.

"Can I help you in some way?" the lady asked, directing her question to Olivia.

Olivia smiled. "Someone stole my phone and we wondered if we could use yours to call a friend to come pick us up. I understand if you don't want a stranger using your cell, but we really need to get a ride."

"Sure. No problem." The woman plundered around in her diaper bag and eventually came out with an iPhone. "Here you go."

Graham stood and walked a few steps away so she couldn't overhear him asking for a couple of bodyguards to go with that ride.

When he returned, Olivia was cooing over the baby and chatting with the woman. She glanced over her shoulder once or twice. Graham knew she was hoping Bernard was gone but he wasn't.

It was odd that the man would continue to stand and stare at the daughter of his wife. What kind of guy did that? Did he think he was so invincible he could just wait her out and grab her when she left the building, and the crowd wasn't around?

Graham handed the phone back to the woman. "Thanks so much and mostly, thanks for restoring my friend's faith in humankind."

"You're welcome." The lady smiled. "I think."

Graham knelt down next to the baby. "You're a cutie, aren't you?"

The little boy reached out and grabbed Graham's nose.

Laughing, Graham said, "You're a strong little dude."

"He sure likes you. He usually doesn't allow anyone near him. You have some kind of gift with kids, don't you?"

"Maybe it's because they think I'm as weird-looking as they are. I mean, really, check him out. He's bald, drools, and can't use the bathroom by himself but women are all over him."

"Your husband is hilarious," the woman, giggling, said to Olivia.

Rather than denying their relationship, Olivia said, "He keeps me entertained, for sure. And just so you know, he does a lot for children. Especially the ones who are ill."

"That's wonderful." She held her hand out and shook both theirs. "It was nice to loan you my phone."

When she was gone, Graham said, "They should be here any moment."

"Can I ask you a question?"

"Sure." He looked at his watch. "We have some time."

"Have you ever come close to marrying or having children?"

"What brings that up?"

"That woman and her son. She was right. You're fantastic with kids. I just wondered if you'd ever wanted any of your own."

"Sure. Of course, but I need the right circumstances, and, so far, that hasn't happened for me."

"Me either."

"No little Bradfords dancing in your head?"

She shuddered. "I should say not."

Graham watched the doors leading in from the skating rink. "Here's the cavalry."

"Oh no, Roberts is with them. I thought you didn't want to see him again."

"Ever heard that phrase about sleeping with the enemy? I won't be doing exactly that, but if we're going to get you out of here and to that press conference, we can't be too picky about our rescuers."

"That's true."

The four men stepped over to their table. Roberts was the one to speak. "We have a car at the curb. It's running with the driver in place. We told the valet that we were picking up some VIPs so act important."

Graham shook his head. Did Roberts have to make it so dramatic? "Just get her out of here in one piece and past the big guy over there standing with the man in the three-thousand dollar suit."

"No problem." Robert's led the way with a bodyguard on either side of Olivia and the fourth man behind her. They walked toward the exit in that formation. Graham followed. Letting them get a little ahead as he limped along, his blasted leg acting up again.

When they were almost to the door, someone stepped in sync with Graham. He turned to see who it was. A gun poked into his ribcage.

⌘

When they got to the limo at the curb, Olivia was assisted into the back seat.

Expecting Graham to be right behind her, she glanced out at the street when the four men got in behind her. He was nowhere to be seen.

"Where's Graham?"

"I don't know. He was right there last I saw. I'm sorry, Miss Jacobs, we can't wait for him. We need to get you to Hofstra's office and into the suit he's borrowed for you to wear to the conference. We have someone to do your hair as well. He wants to present a polished front to the television audience."

"But what about Graham? We can't just leave him." Olivia tried to open the door, but one of the guards stopped her.

"We don't need him. We need you. He's a big boy. He can find his own way to either the office or back to the hotel where you're staying."

"I can't believe you. He was in the army with you, and you'd abandon him?" She knew she was acting like a shrew, but she couldn't believe they would leave him. What kind of person did that? It was unthinkable.

The limo pulled into traffic.

"He may have been in my unit, but I've already saved his ungrateful hide once. Why should I keep doing it?"

"I don't know. Maybe because you're a human being with respect for others?"

"Look, lady, I was asked to get some guards to protect you by Graham and was asked by my boss, Mr. Hofstra, to bring you to him for a press conference. The way I see it, I've done what I was required to do."

"Well, I don't have to cooperate with the press conference, and I'm putting you on notice right now that unless and until I see Graham again—and he's in one piece—I won't say one word." She crossed her arms. Acting as if she were mad but really being terrified Graham had been grabbed by Bernard for leverage against her, she hid her hands near her armpits so the men in the limo couldn't see them shaking.

Her whole being was vibrating with terror for Graham. There was no way Bernard would let him go if he had him. Unless she gave herself up. Could she do it? After all Graham did to try to help her, could she allow Bernard to win by walking into his house and letting him do what he wanted to her in exchange for Graham's life?

In that moment, moving toward Columbus Circle, she knew. Yes. She could do it. Graham Rockford had worked his way into her heart with his quiet, yet strong, way and she could and would gladly sacrifice herself for him.

As soon as she could get away from this, her new captor.

When they arrived at Hofstra's building, Olivia sat in the car after the three guards stepped out.

Roberts glared at her. "Do you think you're merely going to stay here in Mr. Hofstra's limo all night? You can't, you know. You have to come inside. There's really no choice."

"I don't owe Mr. Hofstra anything."

"You sure do. Did you forget we just got you away from Bernard? Safely away, I may add."

"But you didn't get Graham out. He's there in the clutches of the most unethical man I've ever met. He could be killed, and this was not our deal. Not at all." She shook her head.

"Look, Graham Rockford has survived a lot worse than that old jerk married to your mother. You'll see, he's going to be fine."

"You don't know that. At all." Her heart hurt. It threatened to burst out of her chest.

"I would wager on it." Roberts held his hand out. "Let's get this press conference done and then I'll personally go with you to find Rockford. How's that for a deal?"

"It's not a deal, and I'm tempted to walk out of this vehicle and stroll into Central Park. Maybe throw myself prostrate onto the Imagine memorial to Lennon and let whoever wants to either kill me or haul me off to jail have their way with it."

"Why would they haul you to jail?" Roberts sneered. "You haven't broken any laws, have you?"

"Sure, I did. Didn't you read the tabloids? I whacked some guys in Texas." A hysterical laugh burst from her. Olivia hugged her arms across her body and rocked back and forth.

Roberts reached out and smacked her. "Calm down."

Stunned, she sobered instantly and gaped at him. "What the hell?"

"It's what's done for hysteria." He stared at her for a

moment. "And now that you're all right, let's get upstairs and get this done." Leaning forward, he touched her knee. "I *do* love Rockford, and even though he wasn't kind to me earlier, we're brothers in arms. I swear to you, I'll help him as soon as my duty to Hofstra is over for the evening."

"And what if that's too late?"

"Not to be negative, but what if it's already too late?"

"If it is, then it's on your head." Olivia's voice shook. "On yours, your goons, and Mr. Hofstra's. And I won't stop until you all pay."

Roberts gave a curt nod. "Fair enough."

With reluctance, she had to face it. Graham could already be hurt or dead, and there was not one thing she could do about it. She slid out of the back seat.

Upstairs, she allowed herself to be dressed in a hideous suit that clashed with her hair and complexion. She was sure she would look a fright on television, but she really didn't care one iota. All she could focus on was Graham.

How she would be able to stand there and pretend to be calm while Hofstra made his announcement about his investigation, she didn't know.

While her make-up was being done, Jonathan Hofstra came into the room. "Are you ready? It's almost show time."

"Yes. Have you found anything out yet?"

"No. I was hoping for something by airtime but so far, no call."

As if the words conjured the phone to ring, a young woman stepped up to Mr. Hofstra with a cell. "There's a call for you, sir."

He snatched the phone from her and placed it to his ear. "Hofstra."

Olivia watched as he listened to whoever was on the other end. His face got redder as the conversation went on. Finally, he said, "You're not going to intimidate me, and for your information, all my calls are recorded as I'm sure you heard when you—or if you—listened while you were on hold before I picked up. If you try anything, this call will be made public."

He paused again while the other person spoke.

Olivia, anxious to hear what was being said, leaned forward as if that would help her understand the garbled words coming from the other end of the line.

No such luck. She couldn't tell one thing that was going on.

Finally, Hofstra ended the call. He grinned slyly at her. "We've got Bernard on the run. He's got his cronies calling me trying to stop the press conference."

"Did they say anything about Graham?" Her stomach clenched. Maybe they'd said he was okay.

"Who?'

Now, this was too much. The man was kidding, right? Her blood pressure rose, and her veins were on fire. The blood flow rushed to her ears. "My friend. The one who came with me this morning? The one who called you from Rockefeller Center? You're not a stupid man. Stop playing games with me."

She half-rose from her seat, ready to lay into him. She almost wished she had her wrench. Not that she was a violent woman.

"Oh, you mean Rockford? Sorry. I didn't know his first name."

Like hell. She had no doubt both she and Graham had been thoroughly investigated by Hofstra's staff since that morning. "I'm tired of your games, Mr. Hofstra. I'm not sure whatever help you think you can give is worth playing along."

"All of politics is a game, and your best chance at winning it is to stick with me."

"You don't care at all about me, Graham or my mother."

"I didn't know it was a requirement that I care. I thought we were mutually assisting each other."

"Then let's get it done." Olivia stood and walked out of the temporary dressing area that had been blocked off in the back of the man's office.

She stepped onto the makeshift set and stood to the left, behind the podium she presumed Hofstra would use. There were a couple of other men in suits hanging around.

"Time to get started. Three minutes." The guy in khakis and a polo standing by Hofstra's desk glanced over at one of the suits and added, "I'm going to let the press in now."

The suited guy nodded. "Let's do this."

Hofstra came in and with what could only be described as a wolfish smile, stepped up and took control of the room. Olivia's gut clenched. "Here goes nothing," she whispered under her breath.

Chapter 16

The lights shining in her face almost blinded Olivia. It was all she could do not to squint against the brightness of one cameraman's bulbs in particular. How much more ridiculous would she look with the stink-eye along with the puce suit?

She realized she wasn't listening to a word Hofstra said. Making a determined effort to focus in case he suddenly said something she needed to respond to, Olivia tilted her head to stave off the migraine building behind her left retina.

"…and so, with that being said, I'd like to introduce Miss Olivia Jacobs." Hofstra stepped a little to one side, stretched his arm out to encompass her, and indicated for her to step forward.

Great. With no idea what he'd been talking about, Olivia merely smiled.

"Come on up, Miss Jacobs. I'm sure there will be some questions for you."

Not sure she was going to be able to answer anything

they might ask, it dawned on Olivia for the first time that she should have asked her lawyer to be here with her. Could she be sued for slander for what she may say about Bernard? Geez. Now was not the time to be realizing she needed legal advice. Why, oh why was she so rash? Always so ready to act and not think?

She realized questions were being shouted at her when Hofstra shook her elbow. "Miss Jacobs? Are you all right?"

Olivia shook her head then smiled at the cameras. "I'm sorry. Please bear with me. This is the first time I've ever been in such a position. I'm afraid all the questions coming at me at once are too confusing. Could we have one at a time, please?"

"You heard the lady. Let's have one question at a time." Hofstra pointed to a man with red hair and a mustache. "Lou, your turn."

"Why do you think your mother's coma wasn't an illness? What made you suspect her husband of foul play?" the man named Lou asked.

"All I can say is my mother was fine one day and fell into the coma the next with no sign of any medical issue. She'd previously been perfectly healthy, except for her well-controlled diabetes."

"Why are you just coming forward now?" the next man in the front row asked. "Your mother has been ill for a long time."

"I tried to have an investigation mounted when it first happened, but no one would listen to me."

"And so now you've gotten Jonathan Hofstra to

come to your aid for the real purpose of assisting him in a sensational way to defeat Senator Matthews who happens to be advised by your stepfather. Isn't that right?" the first man, Lou, asked this one and suddenly, the floodgates opened again. More questions were yelled out.

The migraine was in full swing now. Olivia was tempted to walk off and return to the dressing-area. This was getting them exactly nowhere.

"Now, now, you're all overwhelming the lady again." Hofstra leaned into the microphone. "Either you all ask your questions in an orderly way, or we'll have to end this conference."

In response, more questions were shouted.

Hofstra took Olivia by the elbow and led her out of the staging area. As they moved away, she noticed one of the men in suits step forward. He tapped on the microphone as if for attention.

She could still hear what was going on from the dressing room. He sounded like a lawyer and was wrapping up the press conference with advice that there would be another one when any further information became available.

Hofstra plopped down into one of the chairs that had been used as make-up seats earlier. He let out a snicker. "That was wonderful. I love how you acted like you had no idea what was going on. Way to play the naïve, poor little rich girl. That was some great publicity. I bet the senator is on the run."

"What are you talking about? That was a disaster out there. Were you even at the same conference I was?"

"Who are you kidding? That was brilliant."

Olivia shook her head. The man was insane.

"Can't you see? No matter what we find out—even if we don't find out anything—the accusation alone has derailed Bernard and his lackey, the senator."

"*His* lackey? What do you mean?"

"I forget you've been out of New York. Everyone in the know here is aware Lisa Matthews is the pretty front for Bernard. She only acts in ways that are profitable for him."

"As I recall, he didn't have much money of his own. How did he get as powerful as that? On my mother's funds?"

"That and some other interests that have long been suspected of him. The man is slick and slippery. We sure would love to take him down in more ways than one."

"We?"

"Oh, you know what I mean. He's one who needs to be neutralized. If it could be proven he'd done something to your mother, it would go a very long way toward that goal."

Olivia was beginning to believe a lot more was going on than she'd been told. It was clear she'd been used in a much deeper scheme than she'd agreed to. She wished again for Graham to be at her side. He would know what to do. That reminded her. The press conference was over. She could escape.

"By the way," she said, "I must go now. I'd like you to send Roberts with me to find Graham. I don't know where to start looking, but I hope he'll have some ideas."

"Remember that phone conversation I had just before we stepped out on stage?" Hofstra leaned forward in his chair.

"Yes." With trepidation, Olivia waited for what was to come. Dread washed over her. She was unsure why but it was there.

"That was one of Bernard's men. It seems the old bastard has Graham."

"I figured that much as soon as Graham disappeared. Did Bernard's man happen to tell you where they were holding him?"

"Oh, yes. He certainly did." The smile on the florid man's face was terrifying. He had no morals. She could see that now. Hofstra knew about Graham and where he was. The jerk deliberately hid it from her so she would go on with his farce of a press conference. Wanting nothing more than to punch him, Olivia knew she couldn't. His information was too valuable.

"Are you going to share it with me?"

Hofstra rubbed his chin. "Have you a desire to visit the home where your mother is being cared for?"

"Not really. She can't tell I'm there and it would be too dangerous…" She stopped when she realized what he was saying. Olivia leapt to her feet. "Yes. I think I will."

"Do you want Roberts with you? May I provide a car?" The laughter in his voice renewed her desire to smack him, but she refrained.

Making a mental memo to return to do so at her earliest convenience when Graham was safe, she strode to the door at the opposite end of the room from the opening leading to the room where the press conference had been held.

When she arrived, she turned back. "Much as I would like to take you up on your offer, I think I will manage on my own. I don't want to be further indebted to you."

"I'm afraid it's too late for that. I can't let you go alone. It's necessary for me to protect my investment."

"And what investment is that?"

"You, my dear. You." He laughed again. A Snidely Whiplash kind of laugh. Terrifying, really.

Ignoring the threat in the sound, Olivia whirled around and went out the door.

Big mistake.

There were still reporters in the corridor. They rushed toward her, microphones extended.

Before they reached her, the door behind Olivia opened, and someone grabbed her upper arm. She was pulled back into the dressing room. "Perhaps now you'll take me up on the offer of a way out of here and a car?" Hofstra asked.

Clearly, if she wanted to get to Graham, she would have to agree to whatever terms this man wanted. Letting out a deep sigh, she said, "What choice do I have?"

"Now, really, it's not all that bad, is it?"

Olivia didn't even know how to respond to that question. Resigned to whatever was ahead, she hung her head and closed her eyes. Migraine throbbing.

cscs

Graham sat with his hands tied behind his back. The circulation was almost cut off, but he kept moving his wrists hoping to work the fetters loose. Or at least keep his arms from going numb. At a minimum, he could be glad Olivia was safe with the guards Hofstra sent to get them out of Rockefeller Center. For how long, he wasn't sure. One thing he did know about the lady was that she didn't normally sit still for any kind of nonsense. He had no doubt she would be on a quest to make sure Hofstra didn't leave him here in the clutches of her enemy, Bernard.

How she would manage to keep herself out of harm while she looked for him was Graham's biggest concern. If her past behavior over the time he'd been acquainted with her as well as the way she'd handled those jerks at her bar the other night was any indication of how she would behave now, Olivia would be on a quest to make sure he was okay. Even at her own expense. That's what concerned him the most.

These goons were amateurs compared to the men who'd tortured him in the Middle East. Sure, they could kill him, but if they were going to use him for bait to get Olivia to cooperate, they would have to at least leave him alive for the foreseeable future.

And the longer he stayed alert and alive, the better his chance to get out of this with her as well as himself intact.

The door opened, and the man with the massive biceps stepped into the tiny room that had to have less square footage than a walk in closet. The size of the man made it almost laughable to see him squeezed into the space. Almost.

It would be funnier if Graham were loose and could smack the smirk off the goon's face but he bided his time. Hopefully, his turn would come.

"Time to move," the man said as he jerked the duct tape off Graham's mouth with a ripping sound.

Graham tested his lips by moving them before responding. "Where are we going?"

"Does it matter? It's not like you have a choice." The man kicked Graham's bad shin. They'd already discovered that weakness earlier.

Graham winced but didn't make a sound. No use giving the jackass any further impetus to continue to hurt him by realizing the way that affected him.

The man hoisted Graham to his feet, but since Graham's legs were shackled together, he almost fell as soon as he was upright. Staggering and unable to stop his momentum, Graham's body moved backward and knocked the chair he'd been previously seated in to the carpet, taking him with it.

In a tangled mess on the floor, Graham tried to move but he was like a turtle on its back only much worse since he couldn't flay his limbs like the reptile could.

"Oh, good God, must I do everything?" the goon asked as he hauled Graham off the carpet.

"If you would unchain my ankles, I could certainly walk much better." Every bone he knew existed hurt, and it was all Graham could do not to collapse. He clenched his teeth. Keeping Olivia at the front of his mind, he held himself together, knowing he would be needed to assist her when they lured her to wherever they were.

He didn't have long to wait to find out where exactly he was being taken. When they'd first arrived at the place he was driven from Rockefeller Center, he was blindfolded and carried inside by several men. Only when he was in the closet-like space had his eyes been uncovered. It was a dark, stark and gloomy place so he didn't expend much energy trying to figure out where he was.

The goon freed Graham's ankles and led him out into a hallway.

Now that he was out in the open, Graham realized he was in some sort of medical facility. A strange one because even though it smelled antiseptic and looked like a regular hospital, there were no nurses or doctors he could see.

"Come this way. There's someone you need to meet."

Graham, still with his hands secured behind his back, was tugged by the elbow down the corridor. The man stopped in front of a large door. He pushed on the flat metal handle. "Bernard thought you might want to meet his wife. Since you went to so much trouble to bring Olivia home. He's hoping she'll deign to come by and see her mother as well."

"I'm not sure about that. She's smart enough not to walk into a trap." Graham hoped he was right but somehow, in his gut, he knew he was going to be very wrong.

"Don't be too cocky. She'll come." The man's laugh was raspy. He sounded like someone with a short life expectancy. As if he were a life-long smoker. That could be good news.

Graham had been continuing to work his hands and had almost loosened the ties enough to give himself hope of freeing them. He just needed to play it cool and keep trying. All without letting Goon-Head here know what he was doing.

Wishing he knew exactly where this building was and if it was even still in the city, he began to form a plan.

Entering the room, he walked—or was led—to the bed. He couldn't tell which at the moment since he wanted to see Olivia's mother's condition for himself.

When they arrived at the head of her bed, Graham looked down at the lady's face. She was beautiful. Not in the same way as Olivia. They didn't even really seem as if they'd be related. Maybe there was a slight resemblance in the nose area and the body build, as far as he could tell since her mother was covered with several blankets, but that was the only way in which they favored each other.

"She's gorgeous, ain't she? Too bad for the boss that she's been sick for so long."

Graham shook his head. If Olivia was right and he believed she was, the lady was only ill because of the man she must have loved enough at some point to marry.

"She's a real looker. I'd like to have had a go at her myself."

"That's disgusting. The lady is in a coma."

"She wasn't always, you know. I remember her well

from back then. She was always nice to me. I hate to see her like this."

Did the man actually have a tear in his eye? Could he perhaps be swayed to help the woman?

"Do you know what made her fall ill?" Graham kept working with his hands. One hand was oh, so close. It was torture trying to get it out. Well, not literal torture. He'd been there. Done that. Never wanted to go there again.

The man shrugged and ran a hand over Olivia's mom's brow. "I wish I did. I'd love to see her awake again and making the boss toe the line. She never took any guff off him. She was a matron among matrons, and no one got anything past her."

"Were you in love with her?" Graham wasn't sure if asking the question was the right thing to do but really, what could the man do? Either answer him or not.

"Of course not. I liked her, but she's the boss' wife."

The way the man flushed told Graham even more than he expected. Yes, the guy was in love with the lady, and maybe, just maybe, he'd be an ally if Graham tried the move he was going to as soon as he got his hands loose. "I understand." Graham nodded down at the supine lady. "She's a bit too old for me, but I can see how lovely she is. I can only imagine how much prettier she would be if she were awake and talking to us. Haven't you always thought women to be more gorgeous when they're animated and flirting?"

"This lady here never flirted. She's much too dignified for that."

Graham wanted to keep the conversation going. "Can I ask you something?"

"I guess. Even though I could get in trouble for talking to you. I was supposed to drag you in here and wait for Miss Jacobs to show. She's expected to be here, you know. Or at least the boss wants her to come, and he usually gets what he wants."

"You've actually just answered my question."

"What was it?"

"Why you brought me in here to see her." Graham nodded toward the head of the bed.

"I spend a lot of time with her."

"This looks like a medical clinic but where is everybody?"

"It's private. She's the only patient. Nurses come to check on her, but she's alone here a lot. That's why I come. So she won't be lonely."

It was all Graham could do not to shake his head. This guy beside him had been rough and mean for as long as Graham had been around him, even seeming to take delight in hurting Graham's bad leg. And now, as soon as he was in the room with this woman who wasn't even aware he was around, he turned into a lamb.

Graham's right hand slipped out of the binding. Flexing his fingers to get back the feeling, Graham was careful not to allow the piece of cord to fall to the floor. No need to alert his foe that he was free from all restraint.

A quick glance around the room told him they were still quite alone. Graham spied another door on the opposite side of the room. It was near a window.

Supposing it led outside, Graham held back his smile. His plan was falling into place. He'd have to move soon though. There was no way to be sure how long he had. Might as well ask.

"When do you think Miss Jacobs or Bernard will arrive?"

The man looked down at his watch. "Less than an hour would be my guess. That press conference is over, and the boss thinks she'll come as soon as she can get away since she has to know by now that we have you here."

"Do you ever take Bernard's wife outside to enjoy the fresh air?"

"I never thought of it. She's usually in this bed. The nurse turns her so she won't get bedsores."

"Has she ever been in a wheelchair? Can she sit up?"

A sly look came over the man's face. "Why are you asking all these questions about her?"

"I don't know. I figured it was a way to pass the time until Olivia gets here." Graham shrugged. "And I thought it might be nice if the lady got some sun. It's a nice day out there as I recall from before I was brought in."

"It's almost dark now."

"All the better to take her out. After all, we have almost an hour, you said. Why not give her a little treat? I think she'd like it."

"You don't even know her."

"True, but I've been around a lot of women. Being outdoors on a cool fall evening is something most of them like," Graham said.

"This bed *does* have wheels."

Graham nodded, hoping the man would decide it was his idea to take the lady out that door.

In a moment, Graham's prayers were answered.

"Let's do it. We can go out for thirty minutes and be back inside before the boss gets here. He'll never need to know." The goon knelt by the head of the bed and disengaged the brakes. "Open that door, and I'll roll her out."

"I can't. Remember, my hands are bound." Graham made a face and added for good measure, "I'd like to help, but I don't want you to get in trouble for letting me loose."

"You're right. Wait here with her." He walked over to the door and propped it open then returned to the bed. "Follow me. I can't leave you inside alone."

Just what Graham wanted. He followed the man and the bed out into a courtyard.

Letting out a big breath as soon as he realized they were definitely still in the city and even better, that there was no fence holding them in, Graham scoured the area for something he could use as a weapon.

Finding a large piece of wood, Graham stayed behind the man and listened to him talking to Olivia's mother.

He was pointing out a lot of the sights and showing her the colored leaves and talking about the nip in the air.

For a split second, Graham thought he wouldn't be able to go through with what he needed to do. But he knew it was necessary. Vital even.

Pulling his hands from behind him for the first time

in hours, Graham picked up the wood and whacked the goon on the back of the head. He hoped enough to knock him out but not to kill him.

Not that he hadn't had to kill in combat, but this was different. He didn't know what the man had done in his life, but he was at least concerned and caring about Olivia's mother.

As soon as he knew the man was down for at least a little while, Graham grabbed hold of the head of the lady's bed and ran down the street as if his survival depended on it. And it did. To say nothing of Olivia's mother's life.

Chapter 17

Olivia and Roberts rode down Broadway toward downtown. Using one of Hofstra's cars, Roberts directed the driver toward a group of buildings near Battery Park. "I think there's a place along this block where Bernard owns some property. Maybe that's where they took Rockford."

"So that's the plan? Search all the places where Bernard or my mother own land, offices, or apartments?" Olivia asked.

"You have a better idea?"

"I guess not, but maybe if we knew where my mother is, that would help. Bernard *did* invite me to come call on her. I think it's a trap. But if Graham is there, I'll be going straight into the den of the dragon."

Roberts darted a glance in her direction. "You got it bad for my friend, huh?"

"What?"

"I suspect you've gone and fallen in love with my comrade in arms. Am I right?"

She shook her head. "I like him. I'm worried about him."

"And why not add, 'and I love him' because you do?"

"That's not something I'm going to discuss with you." She realized with a shock that Roberts was right, but it was none of his business.

"Saving it for the man himself, I guess?"

Ignoring Roberts, she leaned forward and addressed the driver as he pulled into a loading zone in front of a squatty Brutalist architecture building. "Are we getting out here to see if Graham is in this place?"

"Sure." Roberts opened the door and stepped out onto the sidewalk.

Olivia followed, and they entered the structure. Making quick work of checking with each office's receptionist for the presence of Bernard, she and Roberts dashed from one to the next and soon had the place cleared.

They moved on to the next building with the same results.

Fear grew in Olivia's gut. The longer it took, the more she had to hold back the panic that threatened to send her over the edge.

When they had been in every building on that block Roberts said was owned by Bernard or her mother, she stopped next to the car. "What now?"

"Maybe they're in another one of the properties. Let's check the list I left in the seat."

Getting back inside, Olivia picked up the sheet. "Here's another set of buildings a few blocks north. Let's try there. One of them is a bodega so we're safe in ignoring that one, I think."

"Yeah. I doubt they have Rockford in the freezer."

His comment chilled Olivia to her core. What if Graham *was* on ice somewhere? No. She shook off the dread. She wasn't going to believe he was dead until she had proof.

"Let's go." Olivia leaned forward to speak to the driver. She pointed at a random address. "Take us here."

The driver got them to their destination faster than Olivia would've bet on based on the amount of traffic on the streets. She wasn't going to complain, though. She quite liked that he was able to negotiate the city like a cabbie who'd been there forever.

Exiting the vehicle again, Olivia followed Roberts toward the next place to search. She glanced into the electronics shop they were passing. Surprised to see Hofstra on all the televisions, she stopped and called out to Roberts who was ahead of her. "Look."

He turned and walked back to stand beside her. "It's just the nightly news recap of the press conference."

"No. It's not." She pointed at the screen. "See, I'm not there where I was in the original showing. This is new. Let's go in."

"Suit yourself. I thought you wanted to find Rockford, but if you want to take a detour, I'm along for the ride."

Deciding not to respond since she might smack him, she opened the door and entered the store. This could be important.

"Can I help you with a new TV?" a salesman asked.

"No thanks. We saw the press conference and wondered what was going on."

The man laughed. "It's hysterical, really."

"What is? I never thought Jonathan Hofstra would say anything amusing enough to be called hysterical," Olivia said.

"Not that guy running for office, but that other running guy."

"I'm sorry, but I can't even pretend to know what that means. What other running guy?" she asked.

"Check it out, looks like they're going to show the clip again." The man stepped over and turned up the volume on the closest set.

"…and as you can see, while Miss Jacobs and I distracted Senator Matthews and her advisors with our earlier press conference, a retired army intelligence officer, Graham Rockford, was our boots-on-the-ground man to free Miss Jacobs's mother," Hofstra said. "We apologize for the secrecy from New York's finest, but the mission had to be handled quickly and quietly."

Hofstra stepped out of the way of a television camera. Olivia let out a gasp as she recognized Graham running—more like loping along, really—down a busy Manhattan street pushing a hospital bed in front of him.

In a moment, two police cruisers pulled up behind him with their lights and sirens on.

"Isn't that hilarious? I bet those cops never stopped a bed from speeding before." The salesman almost doubled over in laughter.

"Shh," Roberts said. "I want to hear this."

Olivia stared at him. "I don't know why. It's clear Hofstra is spinning this to be his idea. Anything he says is a lie. Let's go. I want to see Graham," she said, relieved Graham and her mother were out of Bernard's clutches.

"If you mean that running guy, I bet he's still in the Tombs. I imagine they arrested him for taking off with that sick lady." The salesman shook his head. "And if he was what Hofstra called boots on the ground for a mission, he still has to be being debriefed, right?" The man laughed again. "Looks more like cowboy boots on the ground to me."

Olivia had enough. "Come on, Roberts. Let's go call Hofstra and get the real story."

They left. The salesman was still talking but Olivia didn't care to hear what he was saying. She was more interested in how Graham managed to escape his captors and get her mother out of wherever Bernard had been holding her.

As soon as they were in the car, she made Roberts dial Hofstra. She took the phone from him and waited for the older man to answer. She had to wait a few moments for him to go off the air according to the woman who picked up the phone. Once she had him on the line, she said, "Without all the fanfare of that piece-of-crap story you were just spouting on the television, tell me what happened and where I can find Graham."

"And your mother? Do you care about seeing her?"

"Of course, but since she won't be able to tell I saw him first, I think she can wait."

"Your mother is at Presbyterian Hospital under guard. Bernard is already on the warpath with his lawyers, demanding her release to him as her next of kin. We've got a two day reprieve from a judge I know who signed off on the paperwork, but I'm concerned his attorneys will be able to get it set aside."

It was clear to Olivia that Hofstra was going to make her listen to all the information about her mother before he would tell her about Graham. It wasn't that she didn't love and care about her mother, but somewhere in her psyche, in the last few years since she'd lost her, Olivia had already mourned her as if she'd passed away. It was hard to focus on what had been the natural state of things for the recent past when Olivia had a deep-seated need to know what was going on with Graham.

She decided to humor Hofstra to hopefully, eventually, get the information she craved. "What do you hope to accomplish in two days with my mother?"

"The doctor I hired is assessing her as we speak. Trying to figure out what sent her into the coma and, if there's a chance she will come out of it. Wouldn't that be good news?"

"Yes, it would." Olivia placed her hand over the phone and mouthed the words, "Tell him to drive to Presbyterian Hospital." At least they would be moving while she listened to the long version of where Graham was.

"I think you need to visit your mother. I'm going over now as well. Since all the news outlets have our footage, I have some time."

"How exactly did Graham get my mother?"

"Ask him when you see him. He's being looked at by some other doctors at Presbyterian."

"Is he hurt?"

"If you'd get there, you'd see," Hofstra said and clicked off the phone.

Now Olivia really didn't want to make that trip to the hospital. She knew Hofstra was planning yet another publicity stunt. No doubt there would be cameras and microphones as soon as she was let off.

Not seeing any alternative other than asking the driver—who was in the employ of Hofstra—to drop her elsewhere, she opened her mouth to make the request.

"Hang on a second." Roberts touched her hand.

"What?" she asked.

"I can figure what's ahead. My boss is going to want to milk your presence a bit more to bolster his campaign."

"And you have to go along with that. I know. I get it."

"Nope. Not this time." Roberts leaned forward. "Take us around to the kitchen entrance."

Puzzled, Olivia raised her eyebrows.

"I have a sister who works in the cafeteria. She'll let us in, and we can avoid the rush at the door."

"You mean the cameramen at the door."

He nodded. "Exactly."

"But why? Don't you owe your loyalty to Hofstra?"

"I owe Rockford more."

"I thought you saved his life. How does that make *you* owe him?"

"Long story. Suffice it to say it's getting you a free pass past the media."

"I'll take it. Thanks."

The driver pulled into the driveway in front of the hospital but kept going past the normal drop-off place and around to the back of the building.

Roberts got out and tapped on the door.

A woman came out and, after a few seconds' discussion Olivia couldn't hear, the woman left.

About two minutes later, the door opened again, and Roberts signaled for Olivia to come.

Nervous, suddenly, at the thought of seeing both her mother and, hopefully, Graham again, she wiped her sweaty palms against the fabric of the ugly suit she still had on.

Funnily enough, as she realized what she was wearing, she hoped Graham didn't judge her too harshly for the wardrobe choice. She suppressed a slightly hysterical giggle. This was just one more thing to blame Hofstra for.

Olivia stepped out of the car, hoping for the best.

❦

Graham sat in the room where he'd been left by the doctor with a promise to return. He was impatient to get out of the place and back to the office building at Columbus Circle and check on Olivia. He had no patience for waiting around for some doctor to release him. Especially since there was really no reason for him to have been ex-amined in the first place.

Those cops who stopped him on the street insisted he be evaluated even though he was actually on his way to the closest precinct house when he was caught. The plan all along was to take Olivia's mother either to the first hospital or police station he could find. The lady needed protection, and that was the best way to get it for her.

Just his luck some old woman was looking out her window as he broke into a run after knocking out the goon. The snoopy neighbor wasted no time calling the police, and before he got many blocks away, he heard the sound of the sirens. Trying to put more space between him and Bernard's fake clinic, he increased his speed un-til one of the officers yelled out his window that he need-ed to halt or be shot.

"You ready to check out of here?" The door opened to the doctor who was talking as he entered.

"Absolutely. I've got to move on."

"Good news then. You're free to go. Just be careful with the wrists for a while. I've got a prescription for some ointment for the burn marks. You really did a num-ber on them trying to get loose. Use the same cream on those burns on your leg as well."

"Thanks, Doc." Graham took the prescription and tucked it into his front pocket.

"I hope the police get the guy who was holding you. That was crazy. They could really have done some per-manent damage. As it is, there will probably be some mild scarring."

Graham smiled and shook the doctor's hand. "I'm not worried about that. I have quite a collection going."

"Seems to me you need to find another line of work while you still have some unmarked skin."

"Speaking of lines of work, any news on the lady who was transported by ambulance when law enforcement took her from me?"

"They're still working on her, I believe."

"Thanks. From me and her, I hope."

"Me, too. We've got great teams of specialists here, so I'm sure we'll figure it out."

"Good." Graham nodded at the man and asked, "Do I need to sign anything?"

"Nope. You're clear to go."

Graham headed down the hall thinking about making his way to the front of the building to grab a taxi.

He turned the corner and ran right into Olivia.

"Oh, my God, my God. It's you. You're okay." Olivia flung herself at him, almost knocking him into the wall.

He braced himself and put his arms around her. "I'm alive, yes."

She stepped back and stared at his face. "What does that mean? Are you hurt? What did they do to you?"

"I'll be fine. Just got a little roughed up."

"Let me see."

"Do we have to do this here in the middle of the corridor?"

"Oh, sorry." A red flush suffused her cheeks. "You're right. This is a public place, and since we're both kind of infamous now, we should be more discreet." Olivia laughed. "I have to say, if anyone had told me last week that Graham Rockford, a/k/a Rocky, would be running down a Manhattan street pushing a hospital gurney in hot pursuit by the police, I would not have put my money on that bet. What were you thinking and how did you manage to find my mother?"

"Long story and I wouldn't have made that bet either. You've turned me into a crazy man."

"Oh, no, I won't take the blame for that. You got there all on your own, mister."

"We'll have to agree to disagree there." He grinned. "Let's see if we can find where they have your mother and get an update on her condition."

"All right but I want to hear all about where you've been and how you got loose."

"It's a doozy of a story."

"Can't wait."

Graham took hold of her elbow and guided her down the hall toward a nurses' station. "Let's see if we can get some assistance."

When they arrived at the desk, Graham reached out to tap the counter to get the nurse on duty's attention.

Beside him, Olivia let out a gasp.

Curious what struck her as odd, he glanced over at her. "What?"

"Your wrists." Tears welled in her eyes. "What did Bernard do to you?"

"May I help you?" the nurse asked.

"I'm Olivia Jacobs," Olivia said as she leaned in to

whisper to the nurse. "I imagine you've heard the gossip about my mother being brought here after being removed from another facility in a coma."

"Oh, yes, Miss Jacobs, the whole hospital is abuzz about it." She looked at Graham. "Aren't you the guy who did it?"

He ducked his head and nodded, not wanting to get into a big discussion about it.

"You're either incredibly brave or crazy."

Olivia interjected, "He's both but can you direct us to where my mother is? I'd like to see her and talk to her doctor."

"Let me look it up. I'm betting she's on the fourth floor, but I'll check." The nurse clicked some keys on the computer. "Yes, room four-twenty-three. There's a guard on the door, so you'll have to have an ID and be on the approved list of visitors." She smiled up at Graham. "I bet they let you in since you brought her here."

"Thanks," Olivia said. "I'm not sure who authorized the approved list, but surely they will let her daughter see her."

"I don't know, Miss Jacobs. You'll have to check."

"Come on, Graham, let's go." Olivia took hold of Graham's upper arm and pulled him toward the elevator.

As they walked away, the nurse called out, "Come back by if you have a chance."

"Good grief, that woman should've just come right over the counter and laid one on you the way she was flirting."

"She was flirting?" Graham grinned, pleased that

Olivia noticed the interchange. He had eyes for no one but her, but it was nice to be thought attractive.

"Give me a break. You know she was." Olivia reached out and touched his hand as he pushed the elevator call button. "We aren't done talking about those burn marks. I want to know what happened."

"And I'll be glad to share all the details later. Let's deal with your mother's doctor first and then go back to the hotel to clean up before getting some food. I'm starving."

"Sounds good to me. We still have to see what's going on with Bernard as I'm sure he's even more ready to cause me harm now as well as you."

"I hope he's been neutralized."

"Don't count on it. He's relentless. And don't forget, he has a far reach in this city." The elevator came to a stop and opened just as she finished her sentence.

They stepped into the car, and the three other people moved back to make room.

Once they were on the correct floor, Graham led the way toward the NYPD officer standing outside one of the patient rooms. "I think we don't need to check the number to be sure we're in the right place." He nodded toward the cop. "There's our first clue."

Olivia approached the officer and smiled. "My name is Olivia Jacobs, and my mother is the lady you're guarding. May I go in and see her?"

"I have to check your ID against the list I have of people who are allowed inside." He reached for a clipboard on the chair set to one side of the door. After scanning the list, he said, "That name is here. Can I see your ID?"

She shot a look at Graham. "Crap. I last saw my tote at Hofstra's building. I don't have an ID on me."

Addressing the officer, Graham said, "What else can we do about this ID thing short of going back to Columbus Circle to retrieve her bag?"

The officer shrugged. "I have to have a way to know it's really her. I can get in a lot of hot water if I just let anyone in."

"I'm Graham Rockford. Am I on the list?"

"I see you here, yeah. But even if *you* have ID, I can't let her in with you."

"Okay. I get it. We'll be back soon." Graham took Olivia's arm. "Looks like we have no choice. We can get your bag and come back. Maybe we can eat first."

Olivia nodded, and they headed back toward the elevator.

As they passed a waiting area on the opposite side of the hallway, Graham had a thought. "Hang on a second."

He went into the room and shuffled among the magazines and papers on the tables.

Finally finding what he was seeking, he held up a National Enquirer. "Look here, it's the infamous Stillson wrench wielding Olivia Jacobs."

"You're brilliant, aren't you?" she giggled. "Who knew there would be a day I'd be grateful for *that* article? You think that will satisfy the guy intent on doing his job down there?" She inclined her head toward her mother's room.

"I'm willing to bet it will. Or I can have her doctor paged and show it to him." Graham strode back to the officer.

"That was the quickest trip to Columbus Circle in the history of New York City," the cop said.

Graham held up the magazine. "We found proof of Miss Jacobs's identity."

"That's her ID?"

"Yep. Take a look." Graham handed it over.

The officer read for a minute or so then looked up at Olivia. "One thing I learned, other than that you are who you say you are, is not to mess with you. Sounds like you have a mean right hook."

She held up her hand. "Actually, I'm a lefty."

"Go on in but be mindful, my replacement comes on in ten minutes so there will be another guy out here when you leave."

"Thanks." Olivia reached for the door handle and once she entered, Graham followed.

Worried about how Olivia would take seeing her mother after all the years that had passed, he rushed forward to be next to her when she made it to the bedside.

In case she needed him.

Chapter 18

Olivia braced herself. She knew her mother would look older and perhaps not very good, based on the number of years that had passed, as well as the toll her illness would've taken. Nothing prepared her for the way she seemed so peaceful. Almost as if she was already dead.

A shudder ran thorough Olivia's body. Graham put his arm around her. Grateful for the support, she leaned against him for strength.

She felt as if she needed to whisper. True, they weren't in a chapel, but something about the quiet and the eeriness of her mother being so still and silent evoked that atmosphere.

"She looks at peace, at least," Olivia finally said when she found her voice.

"She does. And I can attest, even when I was running down the street with her and hitting every rock and pot-hole in existence, she never moved."

"I sure wish she had."

"Same here, my love. I wanted her to wake up and lecture me about the propriety of me taking her out in her state of *dishabille*."

A bit startled he'd called her my love, Olivia chose to ignore that for the moment. They'd have a long conversation about that back at the hotel, but it seemed improper to do so here.

"Funny that you say that because that's exactly what she would do if she *were* awake. And she would use that exact word for the way she's dressed."

"Somehow, I knew that. She looks like a stickler for etiquette."

"You have no idea." Olivia let out a little bark of a laugh, remembering all the times her mother lectured her. Would that she could do so again. Just for a while, though. Not harp on her incessantly. A little would go a long way.

"What do you want to do? Find her doctor and see what the prognosis is?"

"I think so." Olivia walked to the head of the bed and addressed her mother. "I'm going to get justice for you even if I can't find a way for you to come out of this coma. I promise."

The door opened. A man in a mask and surgical scrubs pushing a cart came in. He turned and immediately locked them inside.

"What are you doing?" Graham asked.

"Putting an end to all this." The man shoved past Graham, whacking him in the leg with the cart.

Realizing, from the voice—even though it was muffled from the mask—and his build, that the man was Bernard, Olivia stood with her arms out, her back to her mother's bed to guard her. She faced the enemy. "How did you get in here? There's no way that officer on duty let you in."

"Funny thing about that, Olivia." Bernard uncovered his face. "I worked it out where one of the men who owe me was assigned to take over this shift. You seem to forget how far my reach goes in this city."

Noting Graham was sneaking up on Bernard, Olivia decided to talk to her mother's husband to try to keep him focused on her and not on Graham. "No, I don't think I ever underestimated that. In fact, that's one of the reasons I left when I did."

"You should've stayed hidden. Everything was moving here nicely. I still had investigators scouring the country for you, and we would've been successful soon. Done away with you on the quiet and then have your body be discovered."

Graham made his move, but Bernard was ready. Without even turning his head, he rammed the metal cart against Graham again, causing him to lose his footing and stumble back toward the wall.

"Stay over there unless you're ready to die." Bernard pulled out a gun. "This will make too much noise, but I'll use it if I have to."

"You've worked yourself into a corner here. There's no way you make it out of this hospital if you start shooting," Graham said.

"I hope it doesn't come to that." Bernard held the

gun on Olivia. "But just in case, I'm going to make sure to keep this aimed at the lady. I don't think you'll try to do anything. You know, in case the gun was to accidently go off."

"What are you trying to accomplish?" Olivia asked. "Mother is here in the hospital finally, and from what I hear, she hasn't had much in the way of medical treatment lately. If you really loved her, you would want her to get better. This behavior of yours proves to me more than ever that you don't care about her and what you just said about my body being found tells me for sure that you're responsible for Mother's condition."

"I am going to finish your mother off, and then I'm going to take care of you."

"And what are you going to with me?" Graham asked.

"Oh, that's the best part, Mr. Rockford. I owe you for helping Olivia escape from Bradford when I sent him down to Texas. He would've had this all wrapped up in no time, and then I could've given my wife a fatal dose of the drug that's kept her docile all these years."

Olivia gasped. There was hope that her mother wasn't ill? She was merely drugged? How could that be?

"Yes, go ahead and be shocked. I've been paying off doctors for years to say she's ill." Bernard shifted the gun in his hand, but before Olivia could make a move, he steadied it and aimed straight at her chest.

"You'll never be able to get away with this," Graham said. He moved to the left as if to get past the cart.

Bernard shoved it at him again, pushing Graham

closer to the window. "Don't make me use this to push you out that window before I'm ready."

"What? Ready?" Olivia asked.

"That's the beauty of my plan. Your mother will finally succumb to whatever illness has kept her comatose with the aid of the super dose I'm going to give her. In your grief, you're going to have heart failure yourself, and then poor Mr. Rockford will throw himself from the window because he's devastated at losing you. I'll be the grieving widower and stepfather."

Graham looked at Bernard from head to toe. "In hospital scrubs?"

"I have on a suit under here. As soon as the officer outside raps on the door that someone is coming to see my wife, these come off, and I'll be crying at her side."

"You have an answer for everything but this," Graham said as he grabbed the side of the cart and rammed it straight at Bernard.

Bernard's hand went in a circle, and a shot rang out. He grabbed a large syringe from the cart with his other hand and ran at his wife.

Olivia's arm stung, but she ignored whatever it was and put her head down to butt Bernard in the stomach. She *had* to protect her mother.

Graham had made it around the corner of the cart and was right on Bernard's tail.

When Olivia's head made contact with Bernard, he fell back and into Graham, the syringe still in his hand.

Stepping aside, Graham allowed Bernard to fall to the floor.

The older man landed with a thud, the gun fell and hit with another bang of a wild shot.

Someone beat on the door and called out unintelligible words.

The beating didn't stop. Olivia's knees were weak, and she was sure she was going to faint. She looked down at Bernard. He had stuck himself on the way down. The empty syringe was poking out of his leg. He was having muscle spasms or something. Olivia wasn't sure. Her eyes didn't want to focus.

"Graham," she said.

He was opening the door. The room filled with people.

"Graham," she said again as she slid to the floor beside Bernard. Her hand broke her fall, but there was something slimy under it as it hit the floor. She lifted it close to her face. Why was it red? What was going on?

The room got darker somehow. It seemed as if someone were turning off the lights from far away. First from the outer edges then closer in.

"Olivia?"

Startled, she tried to look toward the sound of her mother's voice, but she was just too tired. Too, too tired.

❧❦❧

When Bernard went down, Graham opened the door to the hallway. As the room filled, he heard his name called weakly from near the bed. He turned.

As soon as he saw the blood all over Olivia, he ran to

her, berating himself on the way. How had he not noticed the bullet had hit her? He thought it went wild and maybe struck the ceiling or a wall.

He scooped her into his arms. She smiled weakly up at him. "How's my mother? I heard her."

Graham didn't look away to check. He was totally focused on Olivia. He called out, "Get someone over here. She's been shot."

A doctor dashed over, knelt beside Olivia, and looked her over. "Get a gurney over here."

Graham blocked out the chaos swirling in the room as he stared down at Olivia. He couldn't help himself, he had to say it. "I love you, Olivia. Don't leave me now. Please."

She didn't respond.

Two orderlies came in with a gurney and got her on it. As soon as they had, the doctor turned to Graham. "Are you her next of kin? Can you sign the consent to operate?"

"Operate?"

"She's been hit. In the arm. The bullet's still in there as there's no exit wound. We need to get it out. Like now."

"I'm not her next of kin." Much as he suddenly realized he wanted to be, he wasn't.

"But I am," a voice behind them said.

Graham stared at the woman in the bed. She was sitting up and awake. It wasn't like she was the picture of health and rosy-cheeked, but she was definitely awake and aware. And very dignified.

"What do you need signed?" she asked in an upper-class clipped tone.

One of the orderlies placed a clipboard in front of her and, once she signed, the two men, followed by the doctor, left the room in a hurry.

Torn about whether to follow or stay to see what exactly was going on, Graham stood in indecision.

"You may go after her in a few moments, young man, but I would like to know what is going on here. How and why am I in the hospital, why is my husband on the floor, apparently dead, and my daughter shot?"

Graham wasn't sure he wanted to be the one in the hot seat being grilled by this matriarch. She was kind of intimidating. Almost as bad as his own mother.

Hofstra strode into the middle of the craziness. "I can explain it all. Let me bend your ear."

How the man got there so fast was a mystery, but Graham wasn't going to wait around for the explanation. "You do that. I'm going to the OR waiting room."

He didn't wait for permission but stepped over Bernard's body, appropriately dead with the fatal dose he'd planned to inject into his wife. Racing down the hall, he found his way to the area where families waited for news of their loved ones.

And Olivia was truly his loved one. He could only pray she felt the same way he did. She *had* to survive. Surely she would. An arm wound wasn't usually fatal. Knowing that didn't make the wait any easier. It still was taking forever for the doctor to round the corner to say she was going to be okay.

Graham picked up a magazine, flipped the pages, tossed it down, and grabbed another one.

When he'd been through all the ones on the table in front of him, a lady seated across from him handed him another group. "Perhaps you'll find what you need here."

"I need that doctor to hurry and come tell me some great news."

"Do you want hurried or do you want it done right?"

"Good point. I'm a little anxious."

"I wouldn't have known." The lady smiled. "I find that most of the time here, things work out. This is one of the best hospitals in New York. With all the wonderful doctors and residents here, I'm sure your wife will be fine."

"She's not my wife."

"Yet?"

"Yet." He nodded, pleased that the lady was optimistic in more ways than one. She was exactly who he needed to be sitting with right now.

Deciding he needed to do the neighborly thing, Graham asked, "Who are you here for? Is your husband in surgery?"

"Oh, no. I'm retired and found myself at loose ends on the days I don't play bridge. On my free days, I spend a few hours here, keeping people company. The way I see it, we can all minister in some way or another, and this is my contribution. You'd be surprised at the number of individuals who have no support while here."

"Actually, I wouldn't be shocked at all. I've never thought of it the way you do. As a ministry, that is, but I volunteer at two hospitals in Texas. In the children's wards."

"How wonderful. How long have you been doing it and why did you choose pediatrics?"

Graham wasn't sure he wanted to share his story with this woman, but she was so friendly and open, and, more importantly, she was distracting him from his worry over Olivia, so he did.

"I was engaged once to a lovely girl named Clara. She was sweet but had a lot of emotional issues."

"What happened to her?" The lady placed her hand over Graham's as if she knew there wasn't just a break up.

"She died." He ran his hand over his eyes. "Suicide."

"That's always tragic. I guess she was depressed?"

"Sadly, she was manic depressive. I didn't know when we first became involved. I'd only ever seen her on her medication. By the time she had the first bout with the debilitating depression after I met her, I was already in deep." He looked up at the woman. "I wouldn't have left her anyway."

"I sense that about you."

"She stabilized when she got back on her medications, but about six months after that depression, Clara had a manic period. She called me while she was hyped up and, since I didn't really understand what was going on, we got into an argument. I didn't agree to meet her because I was in the middle of getting the winter feed ready for my livestock."

"What did she do?"

"She got mad and started screaming uncontrollably on the phone." Graham shook his head. "I hung up."

Tears welled in the woman's eyes. "Oh, dear. I'm afraid I think I know what's next."

Her sympathy along with the memories and the stress of Olivia being shot was almost his undoing. He was able to hold it together to say, "You're right. She killed herself. I've never been able to forgive myself. If I'd have gone to her, she would still be here."

Patting his hand, she shook her head. "No. You can't blame yourself. Your Clara was ill. Chances are, she'd have done it at some other time. Sadly, a lot of people who go off their medications harm themselves."

"I know, logically, that she probably would have but I still feel like I failed her."

"And that's why you started going to volunteer at the hospital?"

Graham shrugged his shoulders. "Yeah. I wanted to atone, if you will."

"I get it. But what drew you to the kids?"

"Somehow, I found myself believing if I could make a difference before they got too old, that these children would maybe avoid such a medical condition." Graham held his hand up. "I know, that's not medically sound reasoning, but it made sense to me. Then I fell in love with the kids, and so that became my niche."

"And so, Clara's death had meaning, after all, didn't it? It brought you to a place where you could help innumerable children. That's the way you need to remember her, as the impetus to good things."

Graham smiled at the woman who surely was an angel in disguise. "I'm going to do that. That's a wonderful way to honor her. Thank you."

"You're very welcome."

A man in green scrubs entered the waiting area. "The family of Olivia Jacobs?"

Graham stood. "That's me."

✪✪✪

When she woke, Olivia glanced around, not sure where she was and what happened.

A woman peered down at her. "Welcome back, Miss Jacobs. You're in recovery. Your surgery went well."

"What? Surgery?" Shocked at the rasp in her voice and how sore her throat was, Olivia's hand went to her neck.

"You were intubated, so it's probably not good to talk much. Here's some ice water." The nurse held a Styrofoam cup with a straw in it.

Taking a long, cool sip made Olivia feel a little better. Not a lot but some.

She realized her arm was bandaged and as soon as she touched the area, everything came back. Bernard dead on the floor. The blood under her when she fell and the wild shot that must have hit her. Did she really hear her mother's voice or was that part of the injury? Did she imagine that?

There were way too many questions to be answered. Of course, the nurse would have no idea what happened in that room so Olivia would have to wait until she could see Graham.

She closed her eyes, thinking back over the scene and all that Bernard had said. Bradford came to mind. Would he be arrested on her word he'd tried to kill her at Bernard's request? Would anyone believe any of the story? She'd lived it herself and still wasn't quite sure how to wrap her head around it.

"Don't go to sleep. You have to stay in here until you're alert."

That made a difference. Olivia wasn't planning to sleep, she just wanted to rethink all that had happened that day. She opened her eyes. "I'm fine. Can they put me in a room?"

"I'll call down for an orderly." The nurse stood and moved out of Olivia's sight, but she could hear her on the phone.

Soon, she was moved onto a fresh bed and rolled down the hallway to an elevator and then a room.

After she was settled, the door opened to Graham. Her heart soared as soon as she saw him. He looked as exhausted as she felt. She remembered he was hungry even before they went to see her mother. "Did you eat?"

He shook his head. "You amaze me. You've been shot and had surgery, and you want to know if I ate?"

"I remembered you were hungry. I don't know how long I've been out and was worried."

"Nope. No food yet, but I'll be fine." He stepped over and took hold of her hand. On the side, she wasn't bandaged on. "How are you?"

"Sore but okay. What's happened? Bernard's dead, right?"

"Bernard is dead, my sister is scrambling to save her campaign, Hofstra is crowing all over the television about his great act in uncovering Bernard's nefarious scheme to kill you and then your mother." He smiled down at her. "And the best news, your mother isn't in a coma. She's awake."

"So that *was* her voice I heard when I was blacking out?"

"Yes. It was."

"When can I see her?"

"They still have her under observation, but she's as anxious to see you, so I imagine they'll make it happen soon."

"If I know my mother, it'll happen on her timetable, not anyone else's." Olivia smiled. Yes, her mother was formidable.

"I got that vibe about her."

"You never told me how you found her and how you broke her out."

"Can we save that story for now?"

Olivia realized he still held her hand. "Sure. Why? You have something else you'd rather talk about?"

"I'm probably going to regret this, but I'm compelled to do it."

"Good grief, Graham, what are you going to do?" Her throat still hurt, and her arm was throbbing but his expression was so serious, it scared her enough to dull the pain.

"Never mind." He let go of her hand and stepped back. "It can wait until you're released."

"No way. You can't do that. Fair play requires you to 'fess up now that you've gotten me curious."

"I'm afraid it really *is* a confession," he said.

"There's not much you could confess to that would top the other one I heard today."

"Topping that is something I never want to do."

"And I don't need any more trauma, so if you're going to break my heart with whatever you're going to confess, maybe you should rethink it."

"I'm probably going to break my own heart, but here goes." Graham moved to the bed and sat on the edge. He retook her hand.

Wondering exactly what he meant by his words, Olivia's chest ached. She silently urged him on. Was he going to go back to Texas without her? And would this cause him heartache? What would it do to her?

"Okay, here goes nothing." Graham took a deep breath. "I've been alone for a long time. Never believing myself worthy of finding love again. I've kept people at a distance—other than the children at the hospital—for years. You see, I once let down someone I cared for and so it became easier to be alone."

"I'm sorry. I didn't know."

"It's all right now. I actually met a lady in the waiting room while you were in surgery who helped me understand that I'm not really to blame for what happened. I'll always have a soft place for this former love I lost, but those were a younger man's feelings, not the deep ones I have now."

"What?" Olivia didn't quite get where Graham was going with this. He seemed to be rambling. Or maybe it was the medication.

"What I'm trying to say, in a roundabout way, obviously, is that as we've spent time together these last days on a shared mission and without our normal sniping at each other, I find that I've fallen in love with you. Irretrievably and completely."

She couldn't believe it. He loved her? Olivia couldn't find her voice. He *loved* her?

"I see." He nodded once, let go of her hand, and stood.

"Where are you going?" She reached out for him.

"You look so sad and upset. I want to leave you alone. We can stay friends. Forget I ever said anything."

"I won't. I can't."

"Then I'm really sorry I brought it up. I was hoping you felt the same about me, but I hear you. You can't get past it." He backed up.

Olivia stretched her hand farther toward him. "Come here."

He obeyed and moved toward her again.

She patted the mattress. "Sit."

When he was on the edge of the mattress again, she grabbed his hands in hers. "I say I can't and won't forget what you said because I love you, too. I wasn't going to say anything because I didn't know—"

She couldn't finish her sentence as her mouth was

suddenly otherwise engaged. Graham pulled her toward him and captured her lips with his. He held her a little too tightly, and her arm ached. But she didn't care. Not one bit.

Chapter 19

Two weeks after they got back to Texas, Olivia stood behind the bar and wiped down the wood surface with a damp rag. When she was finished, she tossed it to Sharon. "It's all yours for the rest of the day."

"I can't believe you're going on that motorcycle with Rocky. Prudence. Lord, who really names their cycles?"

"Remember, he wants to be called Graham now."

"Yeah, yeah. I know. More of your influence on him."

"That's not such a bad thing, you know." Olivia noticed Sam at the jukebox. "Don't play that song you know I hate," she called out to him.

"Oh, but I'm going to. It's one of Russell's favorites. He wanted to hear it before we set out for the hospital picnic with the kids."

"How many of us are going? I saw twelve bikes out there last I looked."

"I think we're still waiting for your mother and

Hank. He called and said they had to go back and get something for her hair. She forgot a scarf to put on after she takes the helmet off so she'll be presentable."

Olivia shook her head. Some things about her mother never changed. Even though she'd shocked the heck out of Olivia when she came down to Texas with a guy named Hank, she still had her standards of dress and decorum.

The day she rode up on the guy's huge Harley and jumped off like a kid, Olivia almost passed out. It seemed her mother had taken up with the big goon who Olivia and Graham saw that day at Rockefeller Center.

Her staid mother, the doyenne of New York and the Hamptons, was now consorting with a massive bodybuilding macho man who loved her to distraction. It seemed to act as an aphrodisiac to her mother that the man had been her guard all the years Bernard had kept her drugged. He'd tended to her and fallen in love.

After her mother woke and Hank learned that Bernard had kept her comatose all those years, he'd gone straight to the police and told everything he knew about the man. All of Bernard's shady dealings.

Her mother called him in to see her and thanked him for all he'd done and for allowing Graham to escape with her. When Hank told her he would've taken her away himself if he knew what Bernard had been doing, she realized the man, no matter how brutal he looked, was a good soul and she decided to get to know him better.

When her mother told Olivia all this when she came to visit, Olivia just smiled and shook her head. Lord knew

Olivia couldn't be surprised any longer about the way humans interacted with each other. For her mother to go from a psychopathic husband to a bulky, buff, boyfriend was merely surprising, not shocking.

The door to the bar opened, and Graham walked in. He smiled across the room at Olivia. When his eyes met hers, her heart soared. God she loved the man. He wasn't the most handsome man on the planet but he was hers, and his grin took her breath away. She was sure it always would.

"Are you ready to go? Everyone's out in the parking lot." Graham came over to Olivia's side. "The kids will be waiting. I promised them you'd come. There are a couple of long-term patients who want to meet the lady who stole my heart. I think they believe you may be related to the queen of hearts."

"Wait, wasn't that stolen tarts?"

"The queen didn't steal them. I think she was the stealee, not the stealer."

She giggled and planted a quick kiss on Graham's lips. "I don't think stealee is a word. Please don't tell the kids it is."

He pulled her into his arms and kissed her long and hard. When he let her up, he said, "I look forward to the days when you lecture me on what not to tell our *own* kids."

"It'll take a lot more days—and nights—of that same kind of kissing to make that happen."

"I think I can make the sacrifice. Making love, making kids, making you first my wife and then the mother of my children, yes, that's on my to-do list." Graham winked. A leer really.

"But first, we have a picnic today. Remember, everyone is waiting for us."

"And so we go. But, tonight, when we get back, I say we find a secret room hidden behind a fireplace at the top of the stairs."

"What for?"

"There's a murphy bed up there that really needs to see some action. Poor thing was frustrated the last time a certain couple slept there."

Olivia returned the wink. "Well, we can't disappoint it, can we?"

Instead of answering her, Graham whooped, scooped her into his arms, and spun her around.

As he carried her out the door, she realized Sam was playing that song that always made her cry. Funny thing, it didn't bother her at all anymore. Not at all.

THE END

About the Author

Sherry Fowler Chancellor is a practicing attorney who lives on the beautiful Gulf Coast of Florida. When she's not working on behalf of her clients, she's busy penning a new story or hanging out with her friends and family in their own little slice of paradise.